FRATRICIDE

FRATRICIDE

JUDGE, JURY, & EXECUTIONER™ BOOK SIX

CRAIG MARTELLE
MICHAEL ANDERLE

DISRUPTIVE IMAGINATION

Copyright © 2019 Craig Martelle and Michael Anderle
Cover by J Caleb Design, Typography by Jeff Brown
Cover copyright © LMBPN Publishing
A Michael Anderle Production

LMBPN Publishing
PMB 196, 2540 South Maryland Pkwy
Las Vegas, NV 89109

First US edition, July 2019
Version 2.0, February 2020
ebook ISBN: 978-1-64202-380-0
Print ISBN: 978-1-64202-469-2

THE FRATRICIDE TEAM

Thanks to our Beta Readers

Micky Cocker, James Caplan, Kelly O'Donnell, and John Ashmore

Thanks to the JIT Readers

Dave Hicks
Nicole Emens
Jackey Hankard-Brodie
Daniel Weigert
Kelly O'Donnell
Micky Cocker
Diane L. Smith
Shari Regan
John Ashmore
Jeff Eaton
Peter Manis
Larry Omans
Misty Roa
James Caplan

If I've missed anyone, please let me know!

Editor
Lynne Stiegler

We can't write without those who support us
On the home front, we thank you for being there for us

We wouldn't be able to do this for a living if it weren't for our
readers
We thank you for reading our books

CHAPTER ONE

Etheric Federation Border Station 13 – Under Construction

"Shit! Shit, *shit!*" the construction superintendent railed. "How did we lose another one? What are you stupid fuckers doing out there?"

"Our jobs—building this station. What are you doing in here?" a gruff old general foreman grumbled before stuffing a spiceweed stick in his mouth and starting to chew.

"And that garbage..." The super pointed at the stick. He shook his head and pulled up the incident report that had been flashing on his screen. He read it out loud. "Inconclusive. Safety protocols in place. Probably operator error."

The old man continued to chew as he shrugged indifferently. "Stupid kids you brought in for this job. Making 'em work too fast. In over their heads. You should be ashamed of yourself." He laughed into a rasping cough.

The construction superintendent had had enough. He pointed to the spiceweed stick. "I've had enough of you.

1

You're fired. Get into the receiving barracks until our investigation is finished. You're in a non-pay status effective immediately."

"Suck my ass! If I'm taking orders, I'm getting paid."

"Security!" the super shouted. Two Yollins arrived, followed closely by an Ixtali. The external carapace of the Yollin, along with their mandibles and an unpleasant disposition made them the galaxy's soldiers and security. The Ixtali, a bipedal arachnid species, added to the intimidation factor. "Detain this man for questioning in the latest construction death. I expect he'll be doing hard time shortly for his crimes, whatever they are. Make no mistake, we'll find out." They dragged the cursing and spitting man out, his strength surprising for an oldster high on weed. But he wasn't stronger than the Yollins and the Ixtali.

The construction superintendent mulled over the latest report. He didn't need the running summary to know. The tally was emblazoned in his mind: five deaths in as many months. All gruesome, horrible ways to go. All preventable, at least in his mind. It wasn't normal for workers to die when automated systems did the dangerous work. Someone had to be sabotaging the project.

He sighed. In his mind, he'd already surrendered control, but he needed to make it official.

"I'm turning this one over to the Federation." He poked the request in and hit Send before he could change his mind. As the construction superintendent, the crew was his responsibility. He was angry with himself for not acting sooner. Five lives lost, and he was afraid they wouldn't be the last.

. . .

Federation Border Station 7

Rivka closed her eyes as she enjoyed each bite of every slice of Moonstokle pie. It was the forbidden fruit, delicious for being so reviled. The Earth equivalent was ham and pineapple, but that had been declared taboo during the Queen's reign and was contractually forbidden in the All Guns Blazing franchise. But Moonstokle was not technically the same.

As the franchisee's lawyer, she had determined that Moonstokle did not violate contract terms. She may have been biased, but the pie was so popular that no one complained about the sales.

Her friend, dentist Tyler Toofakre, watched her carefully. He'd finished his burger three slices earlier. It wasn't that she ate slowly, it was that she ate a lot. He waited patiently while she reveled in her lunch.

"No more trips for me. I can't leave my practice like that again."

When Rivka finished chewing, she opened her eyes. "Not what you expected?"

"Unfortunately, it was exactly what I expected. I heard your stories, and my mind concocted the terrors. And then the blood, the fire, the pain, the thrill. It was a bit overwhelming. Keep in mind what I do. Normal everyday stuff. I don't get into firefights. I don't carry dead people. She was really heavy, by the way."

"Don't say that to her unless you want your ass kicked." Rivka chuckled softly, but Tyler didn't see the humor. "There is plenty of room on the new ship if you want to reconsider."

"I just said no."

"Maybe I don't take no for an answer." She took the last slice and shoved it into her mouth while she continued to chew.

"You'll have to accept this one. I'm not going. I will have heart failure and die if I go through that much excitement again."

Rivka looked forlornly at the empty pizza tray. "You did great. You gave us the help we needed when we needed it. With the bigger ship, I'm going to need a real crew with a sick bay that's staffed because... Well. You know."

"Blood and running," he finished for her.

"It seems to be our trademark." She wiped her mouth and dropped the napkin on the table. "I need to get going, see what is on the docket."

"As do I. Lunch break is over."

"Same time tomorrow?"

"Will you order something else?" The dentist watched her carefully to gauge the truth of her answer.

"I will not." A curt reply. Definitive. And exactly as expected. "So what if I do?"

"If you say you're ordering something else, then I'll know it's not you but a doppelganger of you, who I don't wish to have lunch with."

"Strangled logic, but I'll accept it."

Rivka left without paying the check. She'd let the dentist cover it. They traded some of the time unless she wanted to get his outsider opinion. Then she paid. She used a credit stick, although she had no idea how much was on it. Ankh had assured her she would never spend it all. How he knew and she didn't befuddled her.

She strolled out the front entrance of the All Guns

Blazing and headed for the back stairwell. Her bodyguards, Red and Lindy, slipped into formation with her, one in front and one behind. After that, she couldn't see because Red blocked her vision.

"Have you gotten bigger?" she complained.

"Two more trips to the Pod-doc. I had to buy all new clothes."

"Stop getting juiced. You're addicted, and I'm cutting you off."

"Like hell!"

Lindy called from behind, "Defensive much?"

Red stopped and checked the corridor in front of him before turning to face the others. "Nanocytes. For the good of all humanity, a gift from the Kurtherians. They make me better at my job."

"There's a limit, and you just hit it. We don't need a three-meter-tall hulking sasquatch on the team. You are plenty intimidating as you were. Any bigger, and you won't be able to travel with me on other worlds. They won't have transport big enough. I like riding in a limo, not a bus."

"I prefer limousines as well," Lindy remarked.

Red's face contorted. "Just one more. There's extra sculpting—"

The Magistrate cut him off. "You've had your last one. What the hell is going on, Red? Do you think that because you almost died, you weren't big enough or strong enough? You survived! You are fine, and doing the job better than any other human being I've ever met. You and Lindy are unstoppable. And if you get any bigger, I won't be able to carry your sorry ass off the battlefield."

"You're pretty strong for your size," Red countered

weakly while looking at the deck. He wasn't good at verbal jousting. He couldn't defend his position. The Magistrate was right. It wasn't about sculpting, it was about having almost died. "I won't. Lindy can make sure."

"*I'll* make sure." Rivka pulled her datapad from the inside pocket of her oft-repaired Magistrate's jacket. With a few taps on the screen, she declared victory. "Done."

"What did you do?" Lindy tried to look over her shoulder, but Rivka had put the pad away.

"Any Pod-doc time requires my personal approval unless you are already dead."

"Already dead." Red wasn't sure he liked the way those words rolled off his tongue.

"I'm your huckleberry!" Lindy declared. "We'll just have to make sure we keep the Magistrate alive so you can get treated if you need it to keep you from dying."

"I like this plan." Rivka gestured for the entourage to start moving. Red frowned but conceded and headed for the Magistrate's meeting room, where they expected to find Grainger, the leader of the Magistrates.

The Magistrates had the responsibility for interpreting and enforcing Federation law on all signatory planets. There were five of them. There were hundreds of planets. They selected the cases carefully as their influence was limited. Most planetary governments didn't enjoy seeing a Magistrate show up. That meant a failure, something the government couldn't handle. It meant ceding authority to outsiders. That's why the Magistrates operated independently. Hard feelings wouldn't travel all the way to the Federation leadership.

Rivka made quick work of the walk. Red and Lindy

remained in the hallway while Rivka joined her fellow Magistrate.

To find that Jael and Buster were there as well. Chi was on assignment. It was a rare treat to have the five together at one time.

"Friends, Magistrates, countrymen!" Rivka cruised around the table to greet her friends before punching Grainger in the shoulder and taking the seat next to him.

"'Sup?" Grainger asked in his coolest voice.

"Zombie! It's about time you showed up at one of these." Jael shook an admonishing finger. "Gallivanting around the galaxy with your boyfriend in tow, no less!"

Zombie. Rivka's nickname based on her ability to see images in someone's mind but only when she was touching them.

Rivka did a double take. "Boyfriend? No boyfriend."

"Man-candy, then?" Buster Crabbe offered. "Like a napkin, used up and thrown away."

He and Jael shook their heads in unison.

When Jael turned back, she had a question. "So the dentist is available?"

"Say what?"

"I can have him?" It sounded like a question.

"He's not a commodity. We just went through the slave trade, and it didn't end well for the body brokers."

"Is he yours or not?"

"Not. We're friends. That's it."

"I could be his friend..." Jael let that hang. Rivka gave her the hairy eyeball until Jael started to laugh. When she finished, her face took on a hard edge. "We don't get to have anyone who's more than a friend. This is the sacrifice we make."

Grainger waited until the banter was finished before interjecting, "Sounds like everyone has gone through some hard times lately. What we do matters. We care that the Magistrates are capable of doing their jobs. We care that you aren't on the edge of losing it. If you need to take your man-candy to the pleasure moon, so be it. We can't have you out there if you're going to go off the deep end. Last thing we need is a Magistrate gone rogue."

"Like the Rangers were accused of doing?" Rivka asked. The temperature in the room seemed to drop as her peers glared at the upstart newcomer.

Relatively new. She had the best legal education in the group, but she hadn't started where they had. They'd been in the Rangers, more paramilitary than legal, but now only the Magistrates did what the Rangers had done.

"Something like that. Even the perception that we've gone off the rails is enough to have the Magistrates demonized. And then disbanded."

"We've seen it before, and it wasn't pretty," Buster added. The Rangers had suffered that fate. Many of Buster's friends had disappeared.

Rivka met their gaze as an equal. She understood. Red was standing outside dealing with the trauma of his near-death. Lindy was faring better, but maybe Rivka was missing something. She would have to check more thoroughly. Maybe touch both of them inconspicuously and see what was on their minds. It was for the good of the team.

The slippery slope of the end justifying the means. No,

she couldn't touch them without asking first. They deserved to be treated with respect and within the law.

"Are you sure you weren't looking in a mirror?" Jael asked.

Grainger twisted his hands. "Did I miss something?"

"Buster said it wasn't pretty. Jeez, you guys have gone soft. You need to up your game by a whole lot." Jael made a disgusted sound to go with the look she gave her fellows.

Rivka stared back blankly. "So, Bustamove, what are you doing for dinner?"

"He's probably leaving," Grainger answered on Buster's behalf.

Rivka fixed him with her best stink-eye. "After giving us the lecture about how much you care about us, you're going to ship us all out on cases, aren't you?"

"Jael said we were getting soft. Can't have that happen." Grainger tapped his device and dozens of cases scrolled by.

"Those are all important enough to require a Magistrate? What the hell are the locals doing?" Rivka pulled out her datapad to read more in-depth on cases with interesting titles.

"They're probably just like us," Grainger said softly. "Tired and overwhelmed."

"I don't think we're overwhelmed at all. We need to have better cooperation from the locals. That is all I'm asking for. Whenever I show up, they start shooting at me."

"I think it might just be you, Rivka. Anyone shoot at you guys?" Grainger turned to Buster and Jael. They both shook their heads.

"Now that's a bunch of bullshit." Rivka smirked at the group.

A gentle knock on the door.

"Come!" Grainger called without looking. Rivka jumped to her feet and backed against the wall, hand tucked mysteriously into her jacket.

"What the fuck, Zombie?" Jael asked, trying to reconcile what she was seeing.

A server from All Guns Blazing entered under Red's watchful eye and dropped off three large pizzas, deep dish, Chicago-style, loaded with meat and vegetables. A veritable pizza pie.

He glanced at Rivka before squeezing past Red and hurrying away. Red closed the door and returned to his post in the hallway.

"How long have we been here?" Rivka wondered.

"About five minutes." Grainger took the first piece and explored the depth of melted cheese and sauce with his tongue. Rivka made a face. Jael and Buster pulled the other two pies to their side of the table.

"You know I just ate." The smell made Rivka's mouth water.

"So?" Grainger asked, his mouth stuffed with half of a steaming slice. "Peace, calmness and joy. The water flows gracefully over the mossy stones. The wild canabears dip their snouts. Drinking and being at one with the world. Now that your shit is all calm and you're at peace with the world, eat."

"Fine." She reached over, but he pulled the pizza away and sheltered it with one arm. "Why do you want me to beat you into next week?"

"As if you could." Grainger pushed the box back into the

middle of the table. "What do you think about a construction accident?"

Rivka snagged a slice and two-handed it into her mouth. She chewed peacefully.

Grainger tapped her on the arm. "Construction accident?"

"You were talking to me? Why would we investigate a construction accident?"

"New Border Station 13. There have been five deaths in five months."

"What's the norm? And before you roll your eyes, I know nothing about deep-space construction. Absolutely nothing."

"The norm is zero. We don't kill our people anymore when we're building stuff. It takes a perfect storm times ten for something to go so wrong that someone loses their life."

"Sounds like someone has it out for the station." Rivka tapped one-handed, reserving the second hand for eating. "No running? No shooting?"

"No running, definitely. It's a half-built space station. I can't vouch for no shooting. This is *you* we're talking about."

"Thanks for that." She looked through the case file. *Chewing spiceweed. Operator error. Gruesome deaths.* No injuries, just death. That piqued her interest. "I'll take it."

CHAPTER TWO

Federation Border Station 7, Hangar Bay

"Jay, I have a question." Rivka sneezed, and her eyes started to water. Strips of cloth dangled in the hatchway of her "new" ship. The former Skaine frigate had been flushed, cleaned, fumigated, and aired out.

It still smelled of Skaines, a small, blue, and less savory race of beings that seemed drawn to the life of piracy. Their morals conflicted with those of about every other race in the galaxy.

The frigate was far bigger than Rivka's previous corvette. This ship required a crew relegating Rivka and her team to being passengers, but the Magistrate would still fill the role of ship's captain.

"I miss my mural." Jay sauntered down the ship's main corridor, with Floyd the wombat bouncing along behind. Jay had been Rivka's first case. Malicious vandalism on a remote space station. Her parents happened to be the space station's governor. They had called in the Federation as proxies for their failed parenting. Rivka had told them Jay was going to a penal colony and stormed off. She'd brought her on board as an emotional sounding board. Jay had given the Magistrate insight that had made it possible to resolve a pair of difficult cases.

"Has she lost weight?" Rivka asked without pressing Jay on the incense-laced danglies in the entry.

"This ship has so much more room to run around. Floyd is getting the most exercise she's ever gotten." Jay looked away from the strips Red was sniffing and making faces at.

The group stood uncomfortably, no one making a move in one direction or the other. To the right, the bridge, various billets, and work areas. To the left, the engine room.

"If no one else is going to say it," Red started. Rivka gave him a look that suggested he shouldn't say it either. He didn't continue.

Jay's peevish smile made Rivka laugh. "I love what you're trying to do to the place."

"I hoped you would. It still stinks in here. I don't know what it'll take to get the stench out." Jay looked forlorn, like she was ready to surrender.

"That's all I was going to say," Red mumbled. He jumped when Lindy poked him from behind.

"Make way." She tossed a duffle bag into the corridor, then added a second and third to the pile.

Rivka's questioning look drew the answer she didn't want.

"Red's workout t-shirts and jock straps."

"She's kidding," Red interjected, trying not to laugh.

"We have a real gym now. Good job getting us a bigger boat, Magistrate."

"We had to turn *Peacekeeper* in. I still feel bad about that."

"Everyone remembers their first ride." Red clapped Rivka on the back, almost slamming her into the bulkhead. "But this one is better."

"Are you sure?" she asked.

"I am," Ankh said from behind Jay. Floyd nuzzled his legs and nearly knocked him down. He looked up at Jay with no emotion on his face, but she knew. He didn't like animals running around the ship. The cat, Hamlet, had been a thorn in his side, constantly vying for dominance, but Floyd was like a child.

And Crenellians had no tolerance for the inefficiency of play. Ankh stood half the human's height, but with a larger head, making him look unbalanced at all times. He was also a technological genius owing many of his break-throughs to his close friendship with one of the leading Federation researchers. He also had an artificial intelligence, an AI called Erasmus embedded on a chip within his brain.

"What have you done to my ship?" Rivka jammed her fists into her hips and tried to look stern, but failed and gave up after a few moments of Ankh's blank stare in return. He hadn't blinked.

The blue-skinned alien finally listed the upgrades. "Added three miniaturized Etheric power supplies, a Gate drive, a primary plasma weapon, defensive lasers, strategic missiles, gravitic shields, integrated Chaz into the main architecture, and established my laboratory in the engine room."

Chaz, the AI from the *Peacekeeper*.

Rivka nodded appreciatively. "But what about the smell?"

Ankh ignored the question. He pushed past the group and walked to the aft end of the ship, disappearing through the hatch to his new laboratory.

"Three power supplies?" Rivka wondered.

"It's like he upgraded us to be a battleship. You talk about me beefing up, Magistrate, but what about Ankh?" Red waved a hand in the direction of the engine room.

"I'd like to say he's wrong about the upgrades, but we all know he's not. We're like the Marshall Dillon of space. Or maybe Wyatt Earp. I like that movie *Tombstone*." She stared dreamily at the wall.

"Magistrate likes the bad boys," Jay taunted before declaring, "Movie night!"

"Do we have a mission where *Wyatt* gets to show what he's made of?" Red asked.

Rivka gestured her confusion.

"*Wyatt Earp*. Our new ride. Can't call it *Tombstone*. Perps might get the wrong idea."

"That's how it is now? You simply name our new ship? End of discussion?"

"It fits," Red declared.

"It does," Jay said. "I still want to rewatch the movie."

"Me, too." Lindy caressed Red's arm with tender affection. He leaned toward her, smiling.

"What do you think, Floyd?" Rivka took a knee to look the wombat directly in her small, dark eyes.

Wheee! She launched herself at Rivka's face. The team had Federation comm chips installed as part of their Pod-doc upgrades. Floyd had one, too, but even with the upgrades, she had the intelligence and emotions of a toddler.

The chips allowed them to communicate without speaking.

The Magistrate caught the wombat and stood, holding her at arm's length and lifting her toward the ceiling. An arc of puke followed the creature upward before Rivka could stop the lift and put her gently back on the deck. *Sorry.*

Floyd turned around and walked slowly away. Rivka looked at the splatter up her jacket, over her shoulder, and into her hair. "Who fed her Cheetos?"

Jay tried to look away, but Rivka caught her eye.

"Get her something for her stomach, please. I'll be in my quarters." She turned back to Red and Lindy, instantly all business. "Check provisions and loadout. We should have multiple mechanized combat suits on board, along with just about anything else we might need, no matter how dicey things get. We'll be heading to the frontier. Station 13, which is under construction to be exact."

"What about the crew?" Jay asked.

Rivka started to point to the small group in the corridor, but reality came back to her in a rush. "Clodagh, Alant Cole, Aurora, Ryleigh, and Kennedy. They're on board and working their asses off. Between Ankh and Erasmus, their to-do lists are pretty extensive.

"We have a real crew. Chaz?"

"I'm here, Magistrate," the AI said, using the speakers in

the corridor. "I've been monitoring the conversations, and am here and ready for whatever you need."

"I need a shower," Rivka deadpanned.

"I'm afraid you're on your own for that. I'm here for anything else. Not eating, either, really. You'll have to feed yourselves. And workouts. That's on you, too. Maybe I'm not here for much at all. I'll work on my offer of assistance to better align with what I'm capable of providing."

By the time the AI finished, no one remained in the corridor, each having gone their own way to settle in and get ready for the next case.

Federation Border Station 13 – Under Construction

The station mostly looked like the wire ribs of a great spinning top. The top third of the new station was enclosed. The main power supply was at the bottom and operational, providing the energy for the massive construction project.

Bottom being relative, but that was where the artificial gravity generation originated, replicating the weight of a planet in order to pull objects toward it. Thin at the bottom and expanding with the widest section equidistant between the pointed ends. Various hangar bays would eventually accept all but the largest freighters. Those would dock with one of four sealed gantries leading from the station's hangar level.

It was a standard configuration for every one of the border space stations, with minor variations. The construction should have held no surprises. And living beings getting hurt? They weren't involved in anything dangerous since those tasks had been relegated to bots and automated systems.

Yet, five had died. The construction superintendent stood by the window of his office, part of a mobile construction management facility. As in, a spaceship that traveled to major projects, whether new construction or overhaul. The ship had the tools and on-board manufacturing capability to complete nearly any job.

In this case, the smelting and major structural work were being done by a separate three-ship detachment specializing in such production, from ore extraction to refinement. The Ore Lords were first in and first out on any major construction project.

And they were ninety-nine percent automated. Easy money, since they were one of the only contractors in the entire galaxy who could handle such work. They didn't have much remaining for the Station 13 before the smelting and fab crew wrapped up and moved to their next project, but the construction superintendent had asked them to stay until the Federation investigation had time to interview them and inspect their processes.

"What a shit show," Boran Waldin stated for the fourth time.

"You're the safety guy on this project. What the hell is wrong with you?" The construction superintendent wasn't amused. He put his back to the window, crossed his arms, and glared at his safety manager.

"We have the latest processes and procedures in place. The overall risk for any job undertaken by a human or alien is low. Every fucking one is low!"

"Five dead suggest you're wrong."

Boran ran his hand through his hair. He was as upset as anyone. It was his job to ensure the safety of the crew. It was his job to make sure they were complying with procedures. It was his personal responsibility because he insisted on it.

He sat, head bowed and shoulders hunched like the defeated man he was. "I did everything right," he mumbled into his hands, his mind racing as it had ever since the first accident, trying to figure out why. "You can have my resignation."

"Shut your soup sucker!" the superintendent blurted. "*You* are going to figure this out. When the Fed's Magistrate arrives, we're going to meet her at the airlock, all of us, and you're going to escort her and her team everywhere they want to go. You'll arrange anything they want, from casual conversations to negotiations to catered lunches, and you'll stick with them until they're done. If they learn anything, you'll pass that to me as soon as possible, understand?"

"So, I'm a servant and a spy?" Boran wasn't amused, but he had already surrendered. He accepted the premise that no one would ever hire a safety manager with five deaths to his name.

"You are anything I want you to be since I'm paying you. Yes. Spy. Servant. Safety guy."

"Superintendent." Boran uttered the words before catching himself. "You can count on me. When does she arrive?"

"I believe it will be within the hour. Get back to the station. Meet her at Gantry Four. Until the hangar bays are completed, she'll have to dock at an airlock."

"She should be able to fit in Aleph. That bay is ready with contained atmosphere."

"The Magistrate has a frigate."

Boran slumped anew. "I guess she'll be executing people. They wouldn't send the big ship if they weren't going to lay waste to the operation." He held out his hand. "I appreciate the opportunity to work on this project. I'm sorry I failed you."

"Fuck off," the superintendent replied, slapping the safety manager's hand away. "Make sure she has everything she needs. No one is going to get executed on my watch. As soon as she's here, I'll head over. The last few shipments of steel are in a state of flux. I need to break them free, so we can get back to work and finish this station."

"But we're on a safety hold because of the last casualty."

"Then get out there and un-safety-hold it. What are you still doing in my office?"

"I'm starting to think the safety problems are you," Boran said under his breath.

"I heard that."

The manager hurried from the office, shutting the door after himself. He continued to the shuttle dock and waited for the next automated ride. The small spaceships moved back and forth between the construction operations ship and the station. The Great Waldini didn't have to wait at all. The shuttle he had ridden to the construction management ship was still waiting. People weren't out and about because of the work stoppage.

After the shuttle landed in Hangar Bay Aleph, Boran rushed straight for the employee assembly area. He maintained a desk there so he would always be closer to the workforce. They were the reason he was there. They had all seen that he had helped move the bodies from the scene of the accident to the freezer. He had been nearly inconsolable on those days.

Of which there had been five too many. He called up the paperwork on his computer. A box that said the investigation was concluded and identified issues rectified. All he had to do was check the box.

A simple checkmark and the crew could go back to work. He hovered his finger over the box, ready to tap it. Would five become six? He hadn't resolved anything except to identify how bizarre the accidents have been, each unique.

All deadly.

He closed his eyes and dragged his finger over the report on the screen. The box checked. He clicked Submit and turned his system off, then put on his gear and headed into the station.

CHAPTER THREE

Federation Space, The Frontier

Magistrate Rivka Anoa stood at the back of the bridge, the location where Colonel Christina Lowell had personally dispatched a number of Skaines. The area had been cleaned, but it was still something to think about. Rivka put her hand on the wall, but nothing spoke to her. The ship was cold and unfeeling. A tool, but also the body of the AI.

"Chaz, take us to Border Station 13, the new construction site. But not too close. I want to observe it first before we crash their party."

"Of course, Magistrate."

"There's a cat on the ship," Red said in a low voice.

"How did a cat get on the ship? Did the General send Hamlet back to us?"

"This one's orange. And fat."

The person sitting in the captain's chair rotated it until she was facing aft. Lieutenant Clodagh Shortall, the engineering officer, had transferred from the *War Axe* with her boyfriend, Alant Cole, both on a leave of absence from the Bad Company's Direct Action Branch. He served *Wyatt Earp* and the Magistrate as the ship's gopher.

"He came with me. I couldn't leave him over there with those Neanderthals, although he did like the captain."

Rivka nodded. "Chaz, get me Terry Henry Walton on a video call."

A hint of fear passed across Clodagh's face. Rivka winked, and the engineer breathed a sigh of relief.

"Magistrate. Are we going to sue somebody? Because I'm ready if need be." Colonel Terry Henry Walton's face filled the main viewscreen. Leader of the Bad Company's Direct Action Branch, a private conflict resolution enterprise that also assisted the Federation with touchier projects. Terry and his partner, Charumati were from Earth, modified through the use of nanocytes where they were long-lived and resistant to a number of issues that killed most people, like being on the wrong end of a blaster or an explosion.

"No. What? Why would you think that? Is there something going on I need to know?"

"Oh. Sorry. I was thinking about something else. Nothing you need to worry about, but just in case, I'm glad you're just a hop, skip, and a jump away. What can I do you out of?"

"'A hop, skip, and a jump?' Sometimes I don't think we speak the same language." Rivka tried to parse his words but gave up. "We have your cat."

"Wenceslaus? Big orange creature with huge fangs? My archnemesis escaped? Ha! He knew his days were numbered."

From somewhere on Terry's end, a female voice shouted loud enough to be heard. "He's not your arch-nemesis."

"Clodagh brought him over. I just didn't want you to worry."

"Worry? I didn't even notice the evil little beast was gone. I should have. I don't have any furbabies anymore. They've all flown the coop. That would be feathered friends, but you get my meaning. They're all gone. And you've taken more than your fair share! How's my little Floyd?"

"Recovering from an upset stomach. She's fine as long as she doesn't get into the Cheetos again."

"You have Cheetos? Char, why don't we have Cheetos on the *War Axe*?"

"Because your fingers would be permanently orange."

"You're probably right. I love me some Cheetos."

"Are you okay, Colonel?" Rivka asked. "You seem to be talking fast and if I may say it, as your personal lawyer, a bit tangentially."

"It's these young nanos. They're taking me back to my days in the Corps, about a billion years ago. No matter. I'm going to throw some iron around. Damn! Is that Red? What the hell? You look like the Hulk."

"Is that good?" Red wondered, not understanding the reference.

"You tell me. Sorry, Magistrate. I expect you have work to do. Clodagh, Wenceslaus, and Cole. You got one of Micky's best and one of my good people, too. Cole can drive a powered armor suit. If you need that kind of support, load him up and turn him loose."

"All your people are good ones, TH. You wouldn't have it any other way."

"Good hunting, Magistrate. Keep us safe from the evil that's out there."

"Every single day." The comm link closed.

"Interesting," Clodagh mused. "I never got to see that side of the Colonel. He's always so intense and businesslike."

"He has a lot on his plate," Rivka allowed. "But I always seem to catch him off-guard."

"I'm the Hulk? I need to go look that up." Red excused himself, and Lindy went with him.

Another young woman sat up front in the pilot's seat, even though Chaz was more than capable of flying the ship. Rivka introduced herself.

"I'm Aurora. With Ryleigh and Kennedy, we're your flight team. We'll take care of everything related to the ship's flight, in conjunction with your AI, of course. You won't ever have to worry about getting where you want to go when you want to be there."

"Who handles weapons?"

"We will as well. Sixteen-hour shifts when underway so there will always be two on duty at any point in time."

"What kind of combat experience do you have?" Rivka preferred having Chaz in charge.

The young woman winced as if slapped. "None. That was never our job before, but we have been fully trained in systems operations, including over forty hours in the simulator."

"Chaz is a war hero. Trust him before all things." Rivka

fixed the pilot with a look that suggested she would accept no alternatives.

"Of course. We're here to back up your AI."

"Chaz."

"Chaz," the young woman corrected.

"Chaz?" Rivka asked, and when he confirmed his presence, she continued, "Make sure you keep these good people on their toes and up to speed. I want a crew that works seamlessly with you and with each other. Which makes me ask, Clodagh, why are you here and not the engine room?"

"I can do almost everything from up here. Ankh is back there. You've been with him long enough to know that when he takes over a space, he *takes over* a space."

A brief chuckle escaped her lips before Rivka steeled herself. "I do understand." She faced the main screen, which wrapped around two-thirds of the ship's prow. "Chaz, take us to lucky number thirteen."

"I'm sorry, Magistrate, all my research suggests that thirteen is an unlucky number. The issues that have occurred at Border Station 13 suggest that it remains unlucky."

"Bad luck has nothing to do with what's going on at Station 13. I'll get to the bottom of it."

"Hear, hear!" Chaz cheered uncharacteristically. Rivka cocked her head as if waiting for something bad to happen. "I apologize. I got carried away. On a completely different topic, are we taking *Wyatt Earp* into battle anytime soon?"

"I hope not. This is a construction project."

"I can't wait to test the new systems. Ted and Ankh are close to reverse-engineering the alien invisibility cloak, but their version will operate in conjunction with the gravitic shields. Our main plasma weapon is top of the line. Such exciting times ahead!"

"I'll be happy if we never test any of this stuff. I don't enjoy getting shot at."

Shock seized Aurora's features.

"See? You're scaring the crew."

A Gate formed in front of the ship, and they accelerated toward it. In a flash, they were through. The Gate dissipated nearly instantly, and *Wyatt Earp* raced toward a pinpoint of light in the distance. "My apologies, Aurora and Clodagh. It was not my intent to scare anyone. Let it suffice that we are ready should anyone challenge us, as has often happened in our short time together."

Rivka rolled her eyes and shook her head. "Slow the ship, Chaz. I have some research to do. Collect every signal you can and analyze. Tell me what they won't regarding what's going on. I'll be in my quarters."

The Magistrate looked forward to returning to her spacious room. The frigate had been modified to an excessive state of luxury by the owners before the Skaines. The captain's quarters were a multi-room affair with a sitting area, bedroom, separate full bath, and even a small kitchen area. She wanted to install a larger set of screens and one of the recliners like she'd had on *Peacekeeper*.

In due time.

Until then, she wanted to get her head wrapped around the safety regulations and policies she would be investigating. She also wanted to know the people she'd be dealing with. Management led by a construction superintendent named Zack Orbal. A safety manager called Boran Waldin. Subcontractors of all shapes and sizes. The workforce administrator came from the labor ranks. His name was Ossuary Fleener. He went by Oz. The workforce was a transient group that moved from job to job. This was supposed to be a one-year gig, but it was already beyond that. The newest estimate was that construction would take thirty months.

Who benefited from a year-and-a-half-long delay?

Conspiracy theories ran rampant through her mind. She smiled at the thought. The station was under construction. No one had weapons. There was nowhere to run. "Just this once, no running and no blood," she pleaded to no one except herself, hoping her prediction would come true.

"Magistrate?" The door buzzed and Rivka lifted her head from the table. She'd fallen asleep, only for a moment. Maybe longer. She checked the time, but nothing registered.

"Chaz, how long have I been asleep?"

"You presume I've been monitoring your vitals, as in spying on you. I want you to know that I respect your privacy," the AI replied.

"Has Grainger been messing with you again? How long?"

"Forty-five minutes, Magistrate."

"Thank you. What's the ship's status?" Rivka rubbed the sleep from her eyes.

"Operating nominally. We are closing on the station, we'll be docking in thirty minutes, and Red is at the door."

"Come in!" Rivka shouted. She stood up as Red took one step inside.

"No need to stand on my account, Magistrate." He laughed briefly at his own joke. "We're almost on site. What's the loadout for this one?"

"We came here so quickly, I didn't think about any of that. This is a non-combative case, so I fear you'll be bored out of your minds."

"We're here because you suspect someone is murdering people to make some kind of statement. Any time people are killing other people, five, in this case, it's going to be combative. Their weapon of choice may be limited to construction gear, but it's just as deadly as a blaster."

"You have your moments, Red." She wiped her mouth, realizing she might have drooled while sleeping face-down on the table. "Ballistic vests and helmets, non-lethal weapons. Shipsuits for everyone because we don't know if we'll need to be in areas outside of atmospheric containment. Load up, and I'll meet everyone on the mess deck in ten."

Besides the engine room, the largest single space on the ship was the dining area. The rest of the spaces were separated into smaller work areas. The configuration offered enough space to work and live without the crew stepping on each other. It was a relief after *Peacekeeper's* small environs. She'd made sure that Red and Lindy's quarters were on the other side of the ship. She'd heard enough of their amorous interactions to last a lifetime.

Rivka checked her own equipment. It didn't consist of

much. She slipped out of her clothes and put on her skin-tight shipsuit, an undergarment that would seal in a few seconds in case of decompression. It would then provide emergency air for up to an hour. She put a jumpsuit over it, then her Magistrate's jacket as the final layer. The inside pocket contained her datapad and a few of Ankh's coins, which would allow him to hack into nearby computer systems.

As an afterthought, she added her small neutron pulse weapon, affectionately called Reaper, to the inner pocket on the other side of her jacket. Satisfied with how every-thing looked, she headed out.

Jay was the only one there when Rivka arrived. Floyd appeared from under a table, earning an ear and neck scratch before she bounced to a corner, where an oval pet bed greeted her. She curled up inside and was soon fast asleep.

"If we all fell asleep so quickly, life would be grand," Rivka remarked.

Jay nodded before flinching. "Ouch!" She pushed her chair back to reveal a big orange cat licking its paw to clean its face.

"Wenceslaus, I presume?"

"'Tis he, mistress," Jay stated as she rubbed the blood away from her rapidly-healing scratch.

Ankh strolled in, went straight to the food processor, and punched the buttons to deliver something that looked like a corn dog. It didn't smell right, but the Crenellian ate it without comment. The cat jumped to the tabletop and strolled along it, then jumped the short distance to the next table, where Ankh sat by himself.

"You could join us," Rivka offered, but such pleasantries were lost on the small creature. He was who he was, with little patience for anyone who was not a science genius, which was everyone except his friend Ted or their AIs.

"How did you get on board?" Ankh asked the cat before giving his blank look to Jay.

"It wasn't me." She held her hands up with her fingers spread to show that she wasn't hiding anything.

"Shoo," Ankh told Wenceslaus, who laid down and rolled onto his side to deliver a magnificent stretch that filled the table. Ankh was never up for a physical fight, so he moved to the empty seat next to Rivka.

"I'll protect you from your archnemesis," she told him. He turned to face her and stopped chewing. Without blinking, he held her gaze for a solid fifteen seconds before returning to his lunch.

When Red and Lindy entered, Wenceslaus stood and arched his back, hackles up.

"Hey, buddy," Red said in a friendly voice as he swiped his hand past the cat. Wenceslaus slapped his paw against it in a classic high-five. Lindy did the same thing, and the cat slapped her hand, too. They took their seats.

Clodagh entered but leaned against the wall instead of joining the others.

"Here's the case. On the face of it, it seems simple. Five fatal accidents in five months. In our line of work, that's a slow stretch, but in major construction, it is unheard of. One is an anomaly. Five is a complete abomination. That takes us deeper into the world of possible conspiracy, a serial killer, an undeclared war between labor and management, rival drug gangs... Who knows? And that's why we're here. We'll figure out what is going on, and hopefully get the construction of this station back on track. It is important to the Federation, strategically located on the frontier, so it's important to us."

Red shrugged. "So, no running?"

"I doubt it." Rivka smiled. She was happy for such a case, although unhappy that people had to die for it.

"What are the odds?" Red looked at Ankh.

"Currently, calculations remain at one to three for running at some point during the mission, but two days before first blood, which is the longest we've ever had."

"Hang on," Rivka started to complain.

"The science is sound. The numbers are what they are," Ankh countered before she could argue. The Federation leadership at the urging of Grainger and their boss, the High Chancellor had started a betting pool on Rivka's cases. Even the head of the Federation and his right-hand man were in on it. The pots grew with each new case, the winner taking half and the other half going to a separate fund. The big question was *when* first blood and first running took place.

The shortest time for one of Rivka's cases had been less than a minute when the serial killer they hunted targeted them as soon as they left the sanctity of the ship.

"Fine. Count me in on the running, but I'm betting no blood. What are the odds on that?"

Ankh's eyes unfocused as he communed with Erasmus within his own mind before coming back to them. "Seven to one."

"I'll put two hundred and fifty credits on that line."

Ankh took a few moments before he answered. "The

money has been moved from your account to our holding account."

"I'm glad you're on our side," Rivka said, frowning.

"Are you sure?" Ankh replied in his emotionless voice.

Red started to laugh. "No blood? That's a ballsy bet, Magistrate. It's almost like you've never been on a mission with yourself."

"*Case*. And fine. Bring one railgun, but Lindy carries it."

"That wasn't my point, but we will most happily bring the cannon." He cheered before giving Lindy a hug.

"Boys and their toys," Lindy claimed. "But I agree. We can't go completely non-lethal. Just in case."

Rivka tapped her pocket and smiled. "Reaper's coming, too." She looked from face to face. "Any questions?"

"Am I going?" Jay asked.

"Yes. I need you to take the pulse of the workforce. I don't intend to grab everyone to see what they're thinking. You also know how to get into and out of places, like when you were wreaking havoc back at your home station."

"That was a different me." Jay flipped her dark green hair over her shoulder. "But I know what you mean. See if anyone is going places they aren't supposed to be to set up the 'accidents.' I'll keep my eyes open. What about Floyd?"

"Floyd needs to stay here because we might have to go exo-atmospheric."

"Normal people say outside," Red noted.

"Feeling your oats, big guy? I can't wait to get you back into a Pod-doc to shrink your big ass down about three sizes."

"Why wait?" Ankh asked.

Rivka looked at him blankly before it registered. "We have a Pod-doc?"

"Yes. The Bad Company parted with one of their emergency systems after seeing what happened to the crew on the last mission," Ankh stated.

"I don't know if I'll survive if I take any more verbal knives in the back. One-to-three odds. Two days. A Pod-doc. And a cat. My reputation has been destroyed."

Red vigorously shook his head. Lindy scowled.

Jay stood up and slapped the table. The cat rocketed off.

"I speak for all of us when I say that I wouldn't want to be with anyone else. Your reputation is Justice. Those who want to oppress others, they're the ones who should be afraid. I know we aren't. You have the best reputation in the whole galaxy!"

"I appreciate the sentiment. Ankh, I know this will come as a surprise, but I think it'd be best if you stay aboard *Wyatt Earp*. We'll call if—"

Rivka didn't finish because Chaz interrupted, "The ship has docked. Airlock is pressurized. Welcome to Border Station 13."

CHAPTER FOUR

Red was the first one off the ship as per their standard operating procedure, SOP. Next was the Magistrate, then Jay, and finally Lindy. Red filled the airlock corridor as he lumbered forward. His size was deceptive. He was quick because he trained that way, but not as quick as Jay. Her speed was enhanced to a level no one had ever attained before, but at the cost of size and strength. If the team needed someone to run circles around a perp, Jay could do that without breaking a sweat.

Each of the team brought a unique characteristic, the most important being Rivka's peace of mind. She could focus on the case because her friends would take care of everything else.

Red stopped at the end of the airlock and gave the welcoming committee a quick visual once-over before stepping aside. The Magistrate recognized the two from their pictures.

Protocol. *Don't greet the wrong one first,* she thought, then stopped herself. They both deserved the formality of a kind word. And with a quick handshake, she'd get insight into her next move.

"Gentlemen. Construction Superintendent Orbal and Workforce Administrator Fleener." She reached for the superintendent's hand first. "We'll get to the bottom of these accidents. You have my word."

His emotions and thoughts cleared him as a suspect. He didn't know who the perpetrator was but suspected it was Fleener sacrificing his own people to make the superintendent look bad. It was a bizarre theory, but that was the only thing in his mind.

She turned to the workforce administrator, the man in charge of the construction crew. While the construction superintendent managed the entire project, Fleener managed the workforce, the flesh and blood component of those who saw the work done.

Ossuary Fleener had an agenda. He also had a well-disciplined mind. She could see that he would share nothing willingly. He was suspicious of Orbal, and that was all she could get during the brief handshake. Neither man felt guilty. Neither trusted the other.

She had hoped for more. *You're getting soft,* she told herself.

"I'm glad you're here. We started back to work less than an hour ago, after our safety hold was lifted. You'll see the workers doing their thing, but all of them will cooperate fully with the investigation." Zack Orbal emphasized his statement with an exaggerated nod.

Ossuary's lip twitched, making it look like he was snarling.

"You could have waited until after I arrived. This

complicates things." Rivka stepped back to appraise the two. They watched her intently. Jay bumped the Magistrate in the tight space where the airlock met the ship's corridor. "Let me introduce you to my team. Jayita, my assistant. And my bodyguards, Vered and Lindy."

"I'm sorry, but you can't bring a weapon onto the station." Orbal pointed at Lindy's railgun. She canted her head and looked at him from the side of her eyes.

"Under Federation Law, Appendix D, Chapter Seven, Section 1, Magistrates are to have armed escorts at all times. For some reason, Construction Superintendent Orbal, wherever we go, someone is always trying to kill me. Always. So we kill them first. I hope we don't have to administer capital punishment while we're here."

"Call me Zack," the superintendent said in a weak voice.

"She gets you, Zack. I for one am happy someone is armed. This place is dangerous because of you!" Ossuary looked like he was ready to square off with the superintendent.

"Enough," Rivka said in a low and dangerous voice. "We will do without your posturing. I'd like to go to the site of the most recent accident and then work our way backward to the first one."

"Where in the hell is Waldin?" the construction superintendent snarled, his anger at the safety manager grossly misplaced.

"Here, sir," Boran Waldin shouted from down the corridor while jogging toward them.

"I'm Magistrate Rivka Anoa," she said to the harried man.

"I'm the safety manager. If you need anything, I'm at

your disposal for the duration of your investigation. I'll give you copies of everything if you don't have them already."

"I have the investigations you performed, along with pertinent policies, procedures, and regulations. I look forward to talking with you more in-depth."

Boran's shoulders slumped, and he looked at the deck briefly before collecting himself and standing up straight, trying to display a level of confidence he didn't feel. Rivka watched the dynamics between the three men, then glanced at Jay, who was intently studying them.

"The most recent accident site, please," Rivka reiterated, nodding at Boran.

"Of course, ma'am," he answered politely. "If you'll follow me, we'll need to stop by the safety office and get some required equipment before we can enter the active construction zone."

"You could shut down construction instead." Rivka poked the bear to see how they acted. The superintendent and the administrator both stiffened at the suggestion, and she relented. "If construction interferes, we'll shut it down, but until then, business as usual."

"We'll try not to get anyone killed today," Boran grumbled as he turned and walked briskly away. Rivka stepped after him without saying goodbye to management and labor. Red bumped into them on his way past. It hadn't been intentional. It was a small space.

Lindy mumbled an apology on her way past, testing the heft of her railgun when she was directly in front of them.

Once they had taken two corners and were far out of

hearing range of the two men, Rivka yanked Boran to a halt.

"What's the real story?" she demanded, still gripping his arm.

"That fucker called it operator error. All five times. And that other fucker wanted me to annotate that it was the first fucker's policies which put the people at risk. But it wasn't the first fucker's policies; those are mine, and they are by the book and letter-perfect. Fuckers!" He thrust his middle finger in the general direction of the docking gantry.

Rivka bit her lip to keep from laughing, but Boran was serious. And he was upset by the deaths. He had been thorough. His conclusion was that the workers should not have died. But they had, and that baffled him.

"We'll get to the bottom of it. I have resources you don't that could make the difference."

Boran nodded. Red and Lindy kept watch within their limited line of sight. The safety manager motioned to keep moving. "It's not far."

They walked no more than ten meters when he stopped and pointed out a window. "Happened right there."

Rivka couldn't see anything.

"We're going to have to go outside and take a closer look." At Boran's confusion, Rivka clarified, "Integrated shipsuits. We'll be fine in space for a few minutes. Where's the closest airlock?"

Boran pointed again. "Close. That's why the surprise. See those two main supports?" He pointed to two I-beams facing each other.

"Did he get in between them?"

"That's what we call the line of fire. No. He was off to the side. He was crushed about five meters up, on the side, when the structure over there moved."

"Just a different line of fire."

"There's no lateral stress on that secondary structure. I've confirmed it with the engineers."

Rivka held up one finger to pause the explanation. She removed her datapad and took pictures, then beamed them to Ankh for analysis. "We'll have our systems people look at them. Continue, please."

He led them to the airlock. Rivka's team pulled their hoods into place and their suits pressurized. Boran put on one of the transient suits located next to the airlock.

"There's no work in this location at present. We won't encounter any bots or workers."

"Then why was our victim out there?" Rivka's voice was muffled through her flexible helmet, and Boran leaned close to understand what she was saying.

"Structural inspector. The work was completed last week. He was making the final inspection before passing it to the next phase."

"As a structural inspector, he would have known the pressures and where not to stand, right?"

"He would have, and he did. He was in a location deemed safe. You can rip out my toenails, and I couldn't tell you any different."

"Do you think I torture people?"

"Just a saying, ma'am. If you did torture me, you would get the same story."

He finished snapping his rigid helmet into place, and

the group crowded into the temporary airlock. "Red," Rivka cautioned.

"Just my stun baton, Magistrate," he quipped.

"Mine's not," Lindy added.

Boran couldn't turn his head to see the banter, but it bothered him. They seemed to be taking it lightly. "That's fucked up," he said before realizing they would hear him.

"Please don't take it that way. We've been shot at, blown up, blasted, beaten, burned, tortured, and about anything else you can think of that you don't want to happen to you. We will get to the bottom of this by giving it all we have, but it's refreshing to have a case where we don't feel like people are trying to kill us. Those weren't accidents, either. We're not just armed, we're armed to the teeth. Anyone comes after us, we'll kill them. Let us have our sense of peace and any humor we can scrape from a shitty situation because it's the only way we can retain our sanity." Rivka wanted to be perfectly clear with the safety manager.

The airlock door opened before Boran could reply, so he pushed himself through and floated out the door, turning so Rivka could see his face. "For me, this is my whole life. I don't see anything else but the universe closing in on me, crushing me as tightly as those girders did to Jones. I am sorry, Magistrate. I didn't put myself in your shoes."

"They'd probably fit. She's got some flippers on her," Red said as he followed the safety manager out. The rest tumbled through the hatch once the big man was clear.

Rivka grabbed the line Boran dropped behind him. The others followed, and he used his suit's thrusters to take them to the accident site.

"Right here," he said.

Jay asked the question they were all thinking. "Is it safe to be here?"

Rivka looked up to see where the pivot points were that would have allowed the structure to shift as it did.

Ankh?

What? the Crenellian replied.

I'm going to transmit the images using my datapad. I want to know what kinds of forces were at work to make this accident happen, and how someone could manipulate the energies to make it intentional instead of an accident. We don't have motive or means yet, and probably not even opportunity. This could be a pure accident and the group here the unluckiest in the whole universe.

I don't believe in luck, Ankh replied.

Rivka operated her datapad with one hand, capturing a running series of images for the Crenellian's analysis.

"Where's the pivot point that would allow the movement of this section?" she asked.

"That's just it. There isn't one. Let's go up top." Boran accelerated along the beam to the structure overhead. It looked to be firmly affixed to the station. The only members that appeared to be less than solid had nothing to do with the accident.

Pan to your left and head toward the inner structure, Erasmus directed, taking over from Ankh.

"This way." Rivka gestured with her datapad. Boran turned and hit his jets a couple times to change the conga line's course. As they moved away from the expanded section toward the inner core, they found what Erasmus had seen.

"How did I miss this?" Boran asked.

What am I looking at?

Red moved a cover plate out of the way.

Are you getting all this? Rivka knew he was, but until he told her, she didn't understand why this was important.

"It's supposed to be welded solidly, not on a pin with a hydraulic ram." Boran hurriedly pulled the design specifications up on the heads-up display, the HUD, within his helmet. "That's not how it was supposed to be built."

"It appears we have a bunch of new questions to ask," Rivka remarked. "We can go back inside now."

Boran took one last look at the construction. "This shouldn't do this."

"So what you're saying is, this looks like an intentional effort to create a trap in which a worker could be caught and crushed?" Rivka asked.

"That's a bold statement, Magistrate, but I can't think of another purpose for something like a pin and ram. That doesn't mean there isn't one. This is only the third station I've worked on, but I've never seen anything like it."

Boran checked that everyone was clinging to the line and headed toward the airlock. They squeezed inside and cycled the pressure. When the big green light signaled they were clear, the inner hatch opened. Lindy was first through because they had made Red stay in the back.

"Follow me to my office, and I use that term loosely." Boran walked at a measured pace—quick, but not fast or out of control. He already felt vindicated, and it showed in his stride. He nodded politely as the group passed workers going into or out of side passageways that were in various stages of completion.

The desk in the middle of an open work area looked grossly out of place. To the side was a double-wide locker. He popped it open and produced high-visibility vests and hard hats with safety visors. The last thing he removed were gloves. He handed pairs to the three women before looking at Red and trying to gauge his hand size. Boran held up his fingers and Red matched his hand, but the bodyguard's fingers were twice as thick and half again as long.

"I don't think I have anything that will fit." Boran scowled.

"That's it. As soon as we get back to the ship, you're going into the Pod-doc."

"Bullshit!" Red blurted a little more loudly than he'd intended. Rivka's glare froze the blood in his veins, and he had to look away. "My apologies, Magistrate. As soon as we get back unless you want me to go now."

"Now would be good," Rivka replied, allowing no room for misinterpretation. Red scowled as his mind worked.

"Thank you," Lindy mouthed before speaking out loud. "I'll coordinate with Ankh to spin up the nanocyte program."

Rivka nodded and turned back to Boran.

"Why didn't your investigation find that pivot point?"

"Straight and to the point. Standard safety investigations require drone footage of every square centimeter of the accident area. The drones don't disturb the scene, so they passed over the plate that hid the mechanism beneath. It looked like solid sheeting."

Rivka tapped some information into her datapad. "I'll need copies of those videos."

He pulled them up on his screen.

She removed one of Ankh's discs from her pocket and held it up for Boran to see.

"This is a device that allows my people into your system. I am granting a search warrant for full access. You deserve to know." She put the coin-shaped device next to the monitor.

Ankh, can you access the computer system?

I've been in the system since ten seconds after our arrival. The EI installed in this station was easily swayed.

Rivka picked up the coin and put it back in her pocket. "Seems he's already in and poking about."

"What if I have porn on my computer?"

"You don't," Rivka replied.

"Damn! You're good."

"But *he* does." She pointed to the only other occupant of the space. The creature, a multi-tentacled humanoid, looked shocked and started tapping furiously with at least six of his limbs. "Make sure you turn him in for that."

"Bill, you lame fuck." Boran stormed up to the creature and slapped him upside the head. "Get back to work. Go on!"

The creature flowed from his chair and smoothly departed.

"I can't imagine what Grebus porn looks like, and I don't want to know." Boran glared after the rapidly departing worker. "Fucking Bill."

Rivka crossed her arms and looked across the space. Twenty workstations sat empty, a workforce out on the job where something was going on and no one knew what it was. Red finally started to walk away. Rivka snapped her fingers and pointed to the deck. He stopped and waited.

"I'm going to have to shut the job down until we find out who's behind this. If someone is sabotaging the station, we need to stop them. Before then, we're putting the workers at risk. We need to choke off their supply of victims."

Boran sucked air through his teeth. "The guys are going to be pretty mad. They don't get paid if they're not working." Boran typed up the message he knew too well and hit transmit. The lights in the station flashed with the priority message that work was to stop immediately. No one tried to keep working from that second forward because they weren't getting paid.

"Even on a legal hold?"

"Even on a death in the family. These contracts are straightforward. In order to be non-discriminatory, the workers get paid when they work, and at no other times. If there's a death in the family or illness, the worker takes care of it, but they aren't getting paid when they're not on the job. They won't be fired, but there's less work whenever they return."

"So you put sick people on the job, where they can make everyone else sick?"

"We don't work that close together, Magistrate. Much of the work is done in environmental suits, and the workers all have their own. One worker for every ten bots. Generally, the workforce is a healthy bunch, and we don't usually have visitors, so no new bugs are introduced."

"Which means the workforce that started work here is

the same one that's here now." Rivka's mind had seized on information she wanted to clarify.

Ankh, double-check work schedules with the accidents and find me a list of people who were close to all of them.

The station isn't that big, Magistrate. Anyone could be anywhere at any point in time, Ankh replied.

"Boran, each worker's suit has a tracker, doesn't it?"

"Of course. It's standard safety equipment. Geolocation is verified before the worker starts the day."

Ankh, find out where they store the suit movement data and then perform the check. Look for locations up to one week prior to the accidents.

We'll check.

Rivka smiled. Ankh hadn't anticipated the suit movement data. She had finally been able to tell him something he didn't know. She felt smug, but guiltily so. It wasn't her job to be smarter than her team. Rivka only needed to be smarter than the perp.

"Take us to the next accident site, please."

CHAPTER FIVE

Federation Border Station 13 – Under Construction

Rivka and her team visited all five accident sites before returning. The first and second were vastly changed from the time of the accidents. When construction had continued, the station had absorbed those sites within more superstructure, piping, cabling, ventilation, and finished spaces.

"We'll have to take a thorough look at every picture taken, along with the drone videos." Rivka stared at a spot on the wall as her mind tried to digest everything she had seen.

"Of course, Magistrate. I expect your boy already has all the information."

"Our boy?" Jay wondered and started to laugh.

Boran looked at her as if noticing her for the first time. The expression on his face changed. "You have green hair," Boran stated with a smile.

Red and Lindy gave each other knowing glances. *Is that*

what passes for flirting at a deep-space construction site? Lindy used her comm chip to talk to the team privately.

Jay gave her a harsh look before giggling.

Boran smiled.

Oh, brother, Lindy added.

"Time to go back to the ship," Rivka told the team.

"If there is anything you need, anything at all..." Boran looked only at Jay.

Rivka stuck out her hand. The safety manager took it, and they shook. Lindy pushed Jay in front of her as she headed back to the gantry where *Wyatt* was docked.

Boran looked disappointed by the rapid departure.

"Conduct some training or something," Rivka recommended.

"No can do. Everyone is up to date, and the company won't pay for more."

"The company? This is a Federation station. I'm sure I can approve..." Her words tapered off since Boran was shaking his head.

"Even the Great Waldini can't pull that one off. The station is built under private contract first, then sold to the Federation. The government doesn't have anything to do with this; that's why we didn't call you in after the second death. It was still a private issue. I thought we should have handed over jurisdiction with the third death, but they dragged their feet. Finally, at five, we had the most fatalities of any space station the Federation had ever built. The construction superintendent couldn't sweep things into the garbage chute any longer."

"He did the right thing, but I need your help to figure

this out, and most importantly, stop it from happening again."

"Can you execute the guy who did it?"

"There are a lot of conditions that would have to be met for these to be considered capital crimes. State of mind, *mens rea*, we call it, has to show premeditation and lack of remorse. If the guy, as you named him, although it could be any gender or race, met the criteria for capital punishment, I could execute the criminal."

Boran Waldin looked shocked. He struggled to ask the next question. "Have you executed anyone?"

"I usually only get called in when things are bad, and they are nearly all capital crimes. I have administered appropriate justice. We'll leave it at that."

"You've executed people!" Boran leaned away from the Magistrate, a subconscious move that showed his fear.

"Only the very worst criminals are punished in the worst way. Do you think you have one of those here? Jack the Ripper stalking the new corridors of unlucky number thirteen?"

"I don't think so." Boran scratched his head as he tried to think of anyone who creeped him out. The crew was solid. He'd been with most of them before. Same bunch moving from job to job doing the same work, but for a different main contractor.

"Then we're good. I'll be back with more questions. I already know I'll have many."

"I need to work!" an angry voice shouted. Others joined in chorus.

"It's probably best if you go." Boran headed for the gathering crowd appearing from one of the passageways leading into the area the safety manager called home. "Come on, fellas. She's one of the good guys. She doesn't want to see your dumb ass dead and befouling a coffin."

"Can't feed my kids with no pay!"

"You can't feed anyone if you're dead." Boran blocked the way into the space. Rivka took her cue and headed out. Red backed down the corridor behind her. The shouts grew louder, and the Great Waldini's voice could no longer be heard.

"Sonofabitch," Rivka complained as she started to run. Red turned and ran after her, glancing over his shoulder to make sure the mob wasn't getting closer. They caught up with Jay and Lindy, who broke into a run of their own. The four reached the gantry and ran down the access tunnel without breaking stride.

Through the airlock and secured the hatch behind them.

"How long?" Rivka asked.

"Seven hours, Magistrate."

"Anyone pick that number?"

Lindy sheepishly raised her hand. Rivka shook her head. "Come on!"

"I thought it was a safe bet. I take no pride in being correct, but I will take the credits."

"The High Chancellor had seven hours on the running bet, too. You'll have to share. Sorry, babe." Red tried to sound apologetic but not convincingly.

"The High Chancellor?" Rivka was sure the betting had gotten out of control.

"General Reynolds had an hour and fifteen minutes. Nathan Lowell guessed three days," Ankh reported.

General Lance Reynolds was the leader of the Federation, installed by the Queen before she retired from the position. Nathan was Lance's best friend and confidant, but a leader in the private sector.

"But he bet we'd be running. By all that's holy, I'm a barrister and a Magistrate. There should never be any running. There should be state dinners and dances."

No one had an answer to that except Red. "But you always run. One-hundred-percent-sure bet. Someone is going to clean up if there's no running."

"Terry Henry Walton, the eternal optimist. We happily take his credits case after every case."

"No running!" Rivka wanted her declaration to be true.

"I once heard a Magistrate tell a perp that it wasn't what you said but what you did that matters."

"Fine." Rivka didn't mean she was fine with the resolution, only that the conversation was over. "I think you have an appointment with the Pod-doc, Vered."

He didn't move until Lindy grabbed him by the arm.

"Fine," he parroted the Magistrate's tone. The two headed toward the engine room, turned around, and followed a transverse corridor toward the cargo bay.

"Where is the Pod-doc?" Rivka asked.

"This ship has a large storage area that can also be used as a hangar bay. The yacht will fit in there if you want to bring it along," Jay replied.

"My ship. You'd think I'd know these things." Rivka committed to taking a better tour sooner rather than later.

"You know the cases and the law. It's okay that we know this stuff for you." Jay punched the Magistrate in the shoulder before dipping to scratch Floyd behind her ears. "You snuck up on us, you little fluffball!"

I know! the wombat squealed.

"Come on, Magistrate. Let me show you your ship while you think about the next steps of the case."

"She did what?" The construction superintendent knew exactly what she had done.

He gestured for the super to follow him to a more private space than the public area where the safety manager's desk sat. They moved through a short corridor and into an area that had not yet been built out. Boran closed the door behind them.

"You had to know. You called her in to give you top cover. You know we're all on the same team, right?"

"I always know that!" Zack Orbal bristled.

"Bullshit. This is you and me here. You need to treat me more like an adult. Since the first death, you've pushed yourself farther from me, as if setting me up for a fall. If I go, you go, too. But you know what the Magistrate found? We're not building this station according to the plans. A fixed attachment was built on a pin with a hydraulic ram. How in the hell did anyone sneak that in? That's not safety-guy stuff. That's construction superintendent-level. Who orders the materials and approves the construction, including directing the inspectors?"

"She found *what*?" the super stammered. Boran waited. He wasn't about to repeat himself. Zack's eyes darted back and forth as he searched his mind for anything untoward.

"Everything I know suggests this station is being built to exacting specifications by designs available to every member of this crew."

"That's what I thought, but then who?"

"Fleener," Zack declared.

"The administrator is killing his own people and sabotaging the station? That's the stupidest thing I've ever heard."

"You're out of line." The construction superintendent didn't like to be contradicted.

"I might be the only friend you have in here. If you've been doing something, the Magistrate will find it. If you think you're smarter than her and her team, you are sorely mistaken. She's going to find out what's up, and anyone involved can stand the fuck by."

"What's that supposed to mean?"

"Capital punishment. Mass murderers get executed in the Federation. If you don't have anything to do with it, then calm your tits and calm the workforce. Don't try to play them against the Magistrate. You want her to bring in Federation security? Do you think we need more Yollins crawling around the station and beating people into line?"

"We have too many security people already."

"And it hasn't helped." Boran thought he was making progress with the man. The construction superintendent had been aloof from the outset, but his back was against the wall. That was why he had called the Magistrate. "Get Fleener and talk with the workforce. Don't tell them that detail about the pin and ram, but settle them down. If they try to mob her again, I fear they're going to get hurt. And my job is to keep people from getting hurt."

"I know," Zack admitted. He didn't bother to thank the Great Waldini for the magic of redirection. Or maybe it was the power of good leadership. The construction superintendent was an exceptional organizer, but when it came to relating to the frontline workforce, he was sorely lacking. He had people for that, but they had abandoned him, leaving him swinging in the solar winds.

With construction halted, it was time for Zack Orbal to step up, and he knew it. He only needed to hear it from someone like Boran Waldin, a person he should have listened to more from the outset.

Why hire a professional if he wasn't worth listening to?

The construction superintendent nodded to his safety manager and walked out, the burden of the new station and its issues weighing heavily on his mind.

He headed straight for the common area before using the station's system to locate Ossuary Fleener, a man whose fate was inextricably tied with his.

"Workforce Administrator Fleener is located on deck two in the common meal area," the station AI replied.

"Thanks, Bluto." Zack was kinder to the Entity Intelligence than he was to most people. Maybe he had more in common with Ossuary Fleener than he cared to admit, and that grated on his soul. The construction superintendent decided it was better to start with a meeting in neutral territory than by going to the crews' safe place, their dining facility. Tempers would be hot. He didn't want to get an organic, fully biodegradable ketchup bottle in the head. "Please ask him to meet me down here."

Twenty minutes later, Ossuary strolled in. He was followed closely by a trio of hard faces, workers who appeared to be the thug brigade. Two carried huge spanners, and the other, a hammer.

Zack had to bite his tongue at the smug look on the administrator's face.

"Thank you, gentlemen. This will be a private meeting."

"I don't know if I can trust you," Ossuary said in his slimiest voice. "These three are representatives from the various labor trades. If you can convince them, the rest will fall in line. Meet Billy, J.R., and Finn."

"Gentlemen." Zack spoke strongly, evenly. "Now that the Magistrate is here, we need to cooperate."

"You're not convincing them." Ossuary crossed his arms, refusing to move out from under the protective shadow of his three so-called representatives.

"The Magistrate has the authority to implement capital punishment. If she finds the person responsible for murdering five of *our* people, you can be sure they will pay. Mass murderers don't go to Jhiordaan. They get executed. What if she finds a conspiracy? What if she finds people who are obstructing her investigation by forming mobs and preventing her from investigating? You can bet your last paycheck that when you see her again, she and her people are going to be heavily armed. You don't want to get in her way."

The workforce administrator had heard sensationalized threats before. He was unimpressed.

"We have a killer out there. It's someone we all know."

"Who?" Fleener asked.

"There's no one sneaking around the station. All work is done by workers I hired, and workers you manage. Tell me how it could be someone we don't know." The challenge wasn't something that Ossuary could ignore.

"They were accidents."

"They weren't, and that's why the Magistrate shut down the work. She's not going to allow us to start back up until after she finds the murderer."

"I don't like hearing that word. It sounds like you're demeaning the workforce. I think I'll file a formal complaint." Ossuary looked at his trio of enforcers. They nodded in return.

The construction superintendent sighed long and slow while shaking his head. "Your complaint will go up through corporate channels, and maybe into labor and then legal channels. It'll keep climbing until it gets to the top levels of the Federation, and then if they want to kick it higher, it'll go to the Magistrate. Since she's here, why don't you address your concerns directly with her? You'll get an immediate answer."

"I think I will!" Ossuary puffed out his chest.

The construction superintendent had put Fleener right where he wanted him. Let the Magistrate convince the administrator.

"Bluto, can you get the Magistrate on the comm, please?"

"Of course, Mister Orbal," the EI replied formally.

Ossuary had bluffed, and Zack had called it. The comm signaled that it was ringing through.

"This is Magistrate Rivka Anoa. How can I help you?"

"I'm sorry to bother you, Magistrate, but I have the workforce administrator here, and he'd like to register a formal complaint."

"Let's hear it," she replied.

The super gestured for Fleener to take over. The workforce administrator glared at the man before composing himself.

"Yes, ma'am. I take offense that the construction superintendent has called one of my workforce a murderer. We would harbor no such person here, and request to get back to work immediately."

"There is a murderer running loose on Station 13, Administrator Fleener. And my preliminary analysis suggests the most likely candidate is one of the frontline hands. If you're protecting that individual to such an extent that you are enabling his or her ability to kill people, you'll be subject to being charged with the same crimes, and more importantly, the same punishment as the perpetrator. Do I make myself clear?"

Fleener clenched his jaw, and his lip started to quiver. The Magistrate had played her trump card without bothering to see his hand.

"Are you still there, Administrator? I can only take your silence as an admission that you know who the person might be. As such, I need to talk to you privately."

"Not without representation!" the administrator blurted. Billy, J.R., and Finn had taken an involuntary step backward, leaving Ossuary Fleener on his own. Enforcing labor's rights was far different than harboring a person who was killing their own.

"I'll be right there. Don't go anywhere. And because I don't trust you, Mr. Fleener, I'm bringing a combat unit. You should not have weaponized your crew against me. It makes you look guilty, like you're trying to hide something. I don't like secrets, Mr. Fleener. I don't like those who protect criminals. I will respect your rights, but I will not let you obstruct my investigation."

The Magistrate cut the link.

"Can I get you a cup of coffee?" the construction superintendent asked nonchalantly.

Fleener turned to go, but his representatives prevented him from leaving.

"The Magistrate said to wait here," J.R. said, blocking Ossuary's way by pushing a spanner into his chest.

"But...but..."

"I'd like a cup of coffee," Billy noted.

The construction superintendent pointed to Finn.

"Sure."

J.R. shook his head.

"Two coffees, coming right up." Zack Orbal hadn't taken enough time to get to know the workforce, but he should have. Then people like Fleener would have been allies and not enemies. There had been no reason. They all had the same goal. Build the station on time and on budget, then they'd get the next contract, too, unless they were too difficult to manage. Both men knew they were angling to be out of work sooner rather than later unless the Magistrate could get to the bottom of it by clearing them of any wrongdoing.

The construction superintendent was confident he hadn't been complicit. He wasn't sure about the workforce administrator.

CHAPTER SIX

Onboard *Wyatt Earp*, Docking Gantry Four, Space Station 13

"The cracks have started to appear. They are feeling the pressure we haven't even started to apply yet." Rivka chewed the inside of her lip. "I wonder what changed?"

"You stopped the work," Jay replied, stroking Wenceslaus' orange fur. Floyd snored peacefully by her feet. "That shows you have power. They are starting to flail as they look for ways to get back to work."

The workforce turning on itself was inevitable, but could Rivka manage it to her advantage?

"I know Fleener didn't have anything to do with it. Is someone manipulating him? That's what a good line of questioning will discover."

Jay mimed the zombie hand, Rivka's gift that came through touch, enabling her to see into the individual's mind.

"Or that, but I'd like something I can defend in court

just in case. This isn't clear cut when it comes to jurisdiction. It crosses civil and criminal boundaries."

"I thought it was murder." Jay stopped stroking the cat, and he nudged her impatiently until she renewed her attention.

"I can't imagine what the motive is. Without motive, we lack the intent component. It could be gross negligence that rises to the level of reckless disregard for the sanctity of life. *But*, that section of the station was built to pivot. Why?"

Jay didn't know, and the cat didn't care as long as he was being petted.

Rivka looked at the ceiling. "Chaz, give me ship-wide." She smiled. Her ship was big enough that she couldn't simply yell to get everyone's attention. It was much bigger than Grainger's ship. She'd always been told that size didn't matter.

But she liked having the biggest ship, and she'd even gotten used to the smell.

"Coming to you live from the entertainment room, I give you, Magistrate Rivka *Anooooooooa*!" Chaz bellowed like a sports announcer.

"Grainger is going to get his ass kicked." Rivka stared at the ceiling.

"You're live, Magistrate," Chaz reported in his normal voice.

"Thank you. Private Cole, please suit up. We're returning to the station in full combat mode. Lindy and Red, you guys too. Load up."

"Red is still in the Pod-doc. It's taking a little longer

than expected because there was a lot of stuff to undo," Lindy replied.

"How much longer, Ankh?"

"Another hour," the Crenellian answered.

"We go without him. Full load, Lindy. Leaving as soon as possible. Chaz, have Boran meet us at the gantry corridor. I don't wish to be solo on that station until I can make sure it's no longer a deathtrap."

Alant Cole flexed his armored muscles as he put the mech through its warmup paces. He ran the thirty-second routine. The HUD gave him green lights across the board, and he vaulted through the forcefield that retained the atmosphere within the cargo bay. He floated into space before he activated his jets and flew toward the Aleph hangar bay. He cruised through their screens feet-first, letting the gravity pull him to the deck, and hit it already in stride, then followed the map Ankh had uploaded for him that showed the current status of the station.

He opened the wide door giving access to the station, pounded into the corridor, up an access ramp and down another corridor.

"Gangway!" he projected through the suit's external speakers at a group of workers standing in the corridor. They didn't move, blocking the way with their bodies. Cole quickly searched for an alternate route but didn't have any luck. He dialed up the comm link to the ship. "Magistrate. I have workers blocking my way. Instructions, please."

"We're heading into the gantry now, so you need to get through them. Issue my authority, and if they refuse to move, sweep them aside and continue to marry up with us."

"Roger," the private confirmed. He switched back to the external speakers. "Under orders of Magistrate Anoa, I need you to move aside. I do not wish to injure you."

Someone up front gave him the finger.

"Bold and stupid. Advertising your idiocy for the world to see," he said to himself within the privacy of his suit. The ceiling was high in this area, having not been enclosed because the cabling and other conduits had not yet been completed.

Cole accelerated quickly toward the workers, who held their ground for only a second before diving out of the way. The middle-finger man froze where he was, his eyes as big as plates. Cole dove over his head, hit the floor, and rolled back to his feet to continue down the corridor and away from the workers.

"I'm clear. No injuries," Cole reported.

He climbed one more set of stairs, squeezed through the double doors, and stepped into a corridor beside the gantry. Boran Waldin was already there, waiting. He jumped when the mech appeared.

"What are you?" he asked.

"Private Alant Cole, Bad Company's Direct Action Branch, at your service."

"I told them not to fuck with the Magistrate, but they wouldn't listen."

"I expect they will now." The private cycled through his

weapons systems, showing the firepower attached to the suit as well as the oversized railgun he carried.

"You don't want to fire that thing in here."

"You should probably wear an environmental suit at all times," the private warned.

"Shit!" Boran threw his hands up and wildly waved them around. "Are you going to kill everyone to make sure you get whoever the murderer is?"

"It would make things easier," Rivka said as she walked up. "But that's not how we do things. The presumption of innocence prevails. I will do everything in my power to protect the innocent. It helps if they act innocent, but that isn't required for me to support their right to be treated as such."

She didn't tell him about her ability to read minds, which could have been construed as a direct violation of their right to privacy and freedom from interrogation without probable cause. She wanted to use her ability less, having relied on it almost to a fault in previous cases.

When time was the enemy, she could better justify it. In this case, time was important because an entire workforce wasn't getting paid, but she could mandate an exception from the Federation and try to convince General Reynolds to pay for the downtime. She made a note to herself to send the request as soon as possible, just in case the investigation took longer than a couple of days.

Let's see what our buddy Ossuary has to say about cooperating.

"We're not going to kill everyone. I hope we don't have to execute anyone. Lead the perp away in cuffs for an all-expense paid trip to Jhiordaan, a place where they'll never have to worry about money again. But my most important goal is to make sure no one else gets killed."

"That's always been my goal, but damn, things have spiraled out of control!" Boran looked defeated for a moment before bucking up.

"How many times do I have to tell people that's what I'm here for? We'll get to the bottom of this as quickly as possible. I can't share any details during the investigation, but you'll see what I'm doing. I'd appreciate your discretion." She held out her hand, and he took it.

The super asking him to report. Guilt. Internal conflict. He doesn't want to. No secrets, but secretive. Why?

The rush of emotions from the safety manager caught Rivka off-guard, but she weathered them without acknowledging that she knew.

"Shall we?" Rivka gestured for Boran to lead the way.

Lindy took a position next to the safety manager, while the Magistrate had her people both in front of and behind her. They walked through the corridors without talking, the only sound the heavy clump of the mech bringing up the rear.

It didn't take long to reach the area where the construction superintendent and workforce administrator waited. Three large individuals brandishing oversized tools, along with cups of coffee, stood behind the administrator. The tension in the air was palpable.

Lindy took two steps forward and leveled her weapon. "You'll want to put those tools down," she advised. The armored warrior pounded into the space and hovered behind the Magistrate, his weaponry bristling.

The men looked at the spanners and hammer as if the tools had magically appeared in their hands. They immediately set them on the nearest table and muttered profuse apologies as they stepped away. Two of the men cradled their cups of coffee in two hands.

Putting distance between themselves, and Fleener, too.

The super crossed his arms and leaned casually against a desk.

"You have insight into my investigation?" Rivka asked, moving close to the administrator. He was the same height as the Magistrate and should have looked her in the eye, but he shriveled under her glare. "I asked for a private meeting, but you insisted on talking to me in public. Here I am."

"I've changed my mind," he mumbled. "I don't have any information that will be useful to your investigation."

"Now you're wasting my time, and bordering on obstruction. By wasting time not getting information from you, I'm not getting anything from anyone else, either. I can only assume you're protecting someone. A murderer, for example." She grabbed his arm, knowing what she was going to see in his mind.

It was all about him and his authority. He saw his power, not just shrinking, but disappearing. He was afraid to the point of being nearly incapacitated. His thoughts were a jumble of falling dominoes. None of them criminal. All of them shady.

"You are a pathetic human being," Rivka said before pointing at a far corner. "Stand over there."

He clenched his jaw and looked belligerent, but only for a moment. He caved and did as he was told.

"What do you three know?" Rivka asked. The best interrogations were done individually before comparing answers and learning who was lying. She didn't have time for the normal approach.

She sighed as she found herself justifying using her gift to take a shortcut. Again. The men looked at each other in confusion.

"We've found in three instances that construction of the station has been modified to create deathtraps. We don't know where the trigger was or who pulled it, but the workers who were killed had no chance. Like a fly beneath a swatter, their fates were sealed the second they stepped into the ambush. Do you know who or what could modify construction details as the station is being built?" Rivka explained.

"No," one of the men replied, shaking his head vigorously. "I'm J.R., by the way. We work to detailed drawings. We requisition materials based on a list attached to the work package and then start putting things into place, doing the initial fit-up. The bots execute the final alignments, fit-ups, and welds once a living being turns them loose. The bots are the ones that perform the final construction, from torqueing bolts to welding seams.

"That's what the construction plan says is supposed to happen, but it hasn't been."

"But it has!" another added quickly and defensively. He nodded as hard as the other had shaken his head. "We don't do it any other way."

The third looked at the ground. Rivka strolled up to him and tipped his head up by lifting his chin with one finger. "What do you know that's being done differently?"

Images of the workforce conducting their own fit-ups, torqueing connectors, and even welding.

"You're taking shortcuts," she said matter-of-factly.

"The bots were taking too long to get to us. We needed to finish and move on!"

"What did you do, Finn?" the administrator demanded from the far side of the room. Rivka didn't have to look at him. Lindy took care of it.

"You, shut up." The bodyguard pointed at him until he looked away.

"Did you do anything not to spec?" Rivka asked, still touching his face.

Vehement denial.

"It was better than spec!" He kicked at the deck. "Because we didn't want anyone to know. No one can tell the difference."

"I believe you," Rivka told him. "Now describe what you mean by 'better than spec.'"

"The quality control inspectors would never know the difference. We used auto-welders instead of the bots. Those pieces of equipment can be found hidden in a storage space on sub-level nine." He hung his head in defeat.

Rivka casually checked her pad. Sub-level nine was outside the environmentally-contained sections. "Suit up. You're going to retrieve that equipment, and Private Cole is going with you."

"But ma'am!" Alant protested.

The Magistrate tapped the weapon she carried and nodded at Lindy. "I'll be fine. Accompany Mister Finn to that welding equipment and bring it back to the hangar bay for inspection."

The private held out an armored arm and motioned for the worker to lead the way. The two departed.

Rivka looked from one face to the next. "Superintendent Orbal, I need a space where I can conduct interviews."

"How about right here?"

"Bring the inspectors to me. All of them, and hold them over there," she pointed to a wide corridor, "until I can speak to them one at a time. No one is to talk. Hold them in silence. Can you do that?"

"I have Yollins and Ixtali security guards on the ship. I'll bring them over, and we'll take care of it." The construction superintendent grabbed a terminal and immediately contacted the administration ship to issue the order. "They'll be here in a half-hour."

The workforce administrator started to walk forward, but Rivka stopped him with one finger. "I'll need your assistance, if it is assistance you're going to provide. If you step one toe over the line into obstruction, I will throw you in solitary confinement until I've completed my investigation. And if your pawprints are on anything related to the perp, you'll be going on an all-expense paid trip to Jhiordaan. Do you understand?"

"Why would you let him participate if there's any chance he was involved?" the super asked, twisting his face as he spoke. His disdain for the administrator was growing by the second.

"There's a chance you're involved, yet here *you* are."

"But there isn't," Zack stammered. Rivka touched a finger to her nose. She knew something they didn't. She'd hold them at bay until she could get a lead. Playing them off against each other seemed the best way to keep them busy and out of her way.

"Work it out. You two. Among yourselves. But first, get me those inspectors!"

CHAPTER SEVEN

One of the finished spaces on the station provided the office and interrogation room. It was one level up from the area the safety manager called home. The area had been off-limits to the crews, getting closed when they were finished to keep it from getting cluttered or dirtied as the workforce got creative with storing construction materiel or places to relax between shifts. The inspectors would have gone through the space one last time with the construction superintendent before closing it off until the final acceptance walk-through with Federation authorities before they took possession of the completed station.

It would have to be inspected again, but the super believed there would be no final walk-through if the Magistrate didn't get what she needed. Station workers sat idle, not getting paid, nerves raw from speculation. Rivka hoped the administrator and super would put aside their differences long enough to keep the workforce from degenerating into open warfare while she pitted the two against each other.

She started to wonder about her strategy as their animosity grew.

The arrival of several older members of the crew interrupted her contemplation. They were dressed in dirty coveralls. Two were sweating, but not from nerves, from hard work.

"Are you still on the job?" Rivka asked.

"Of course," the oldest replied, a purple-tinged humanoid with skin wrinkled like a raisin. "We work when the workforce isn't."

It sounded like a tagline for a commercial.

"But the workforce is not working because there is a suspected murderer running loose. That means no one works until we learn what is going on." Rivka dug her knuckles into her hips in her dominance pose. The inspectors seemed unimpressed. One shrugged.

She shook her head and checked her pad for the list of names. She counted eight. Seven inspectors stood before her.

"We're missing one. Is he night shift or something?"

No one answered. She pointed to the older alien, the one who had spoken before. He had purple skin that seemed far too excessive for his humanoid-shaped body. "Where is he?"

"She's finishing up one last inspection. She'll be here right after that."

"Boran, get her off the job now, please."

An alarm sounded. Rivka's eyes shot toward the ceiling, looking for the source of the sound as if the speaker would enlighten her on why it was going off. Her internal comm let her know a message was coming from Chaz.

Magistrate, there's been another "accident."

A female inspector? she asked.

Yes.

Send Cole to the accident site, please, in his armor.

"Lindy, you're with me." Rivka's eyes focused on Mister Wrinkly Purple. "Take me to where she was inspecting. Right now, please."

"Was it..." the older inspector started to ask, his face contorting as emotions flooded through him.

"It was why I told everyone to stop working!" Rivka shouted. The seven inspectors rocked back with the force of her admonition. "Stay here, and no one talks to anyone else. Boran, I know you should be out there starting a safety investigation, but this is a criminal issue. You keep them here, and keep them quiet."

"Not another one!" he moaned.

"More to follow." She manhandled the inspector, propelling him toward the door. He wasn't resisting, but he wasn't moving under his own power, either.

"But...but..." the inspector protested.

"What's your name?"

"Humans can't pronounce it, so just call me Marks like everyone else."

Rivka noticed that he spoke with an accent, but it was faint. "Marx, like that human guy from history?"

"I don't know human history. Marks, as in 'marks up the inspection sheet.' I tend to find more issues than anyone else."

He was finally walking without the Magistrate's *encouragement*. "What is the inspector's name?"

"A human. Sheila." The older alien started to pant. His

tongue stuck out as he huffed and puffed. Rivka glanced at him as they twisted and turned through the corridors, bypassing some construction areas while shortcutting through others. He knew where he was going. She would have been hopelessly lost at that point.

"No sweat glands?"

"Just in my tongue, Magistrate. That's why I pace myself. My co-workers laugh at me."

Rivka shrugged as much as she could while they hurried along. They were almost running. Lindy's long strides made her movements look effortless. She carried the railgun as if it were an extension of her body. Her eyes darted everywhere as she moved, looking for things that shouldn't be, seeking light deep within the shadows.

Rivka did not further intrude into Marks' thoughts as they reached the station's outer barrier and a temporary airlock. Rivka pulled her hood up and activated her ship-suit's emergency system.

"You should probably use a real EVA suit, Magistrate," the wrinkled inspector suggested. "It's dangerous out there."

Lindy flipped her hood down and stood back to let Rivka direct the next move.

Marks pointed out a small porthole-style window beside the airlock. An EVA-suited body floated free, restrained by a single tether attached to an eyebolt.

"I know, but my people should be there already. They'll take care of me." She pointed back the way they'd come. "I'll meet you with the others. No detours. Head straight back there, and thank you, Marks, for showing me the way here."

He waved his hand, the overly long fingers flapping as if only loosely connected. Rivka gave him no more thought. She and Lindy entered the airlock and cycled it, ready to head in the direction Marks had pointed.

"On my way, Chaz," Private Cole replied to the AI through his armor suit's comm. Alant pushed a load of welders within a steel net. Finn was pushing from the other side while wearing a standard deep-space construction suit.

Both the private's armor and the worker's suit lights shone brightly. The station lights were not completely operational yet, and with the G-type main-sequence star nearly two AU away, the light was dim at the best of times. Yet the system was well established, with two habitable planets in the Goldilocks Zone, one inhabited by a race known as the Angobar. Once a Gate was built, the system was expected to become a robust trading partner.

The second planet had colonies of settlers who would provide additional nutritional fodder and raw materials the space station would need, possibly even enough for export. The Federation had invested in the system because it was on the frontier. The Angobar had joined the Federation and signed a deal authorizing use of their system. Everything else was beyond the outer rim of known space.

The star was in one direction and in the other, interstellar wilds. The space station was going to support a deep-space exploration branch for government and private entities. It was going to be the best of both worlds—if the station was ever completed.

"Take this to the hangar bay and secure it. Wait there for further orders. You will not touch any of this equipment, do you understand me?" Cole transmitted to the worker.

"Chill, dude! I'm not in your army."

Cole clenched his jaw and tried to come up with a proper reply, but nothing came to mind besides beating the crap out of the guy.

"All you have to do is ask. I'll drop it at the entrance and wait in the ready room with the shuttle pilots. That way, I can grab a chocolate shake."

The thought of subterfuge disappeared as Cole contemplated the drink. "You have shakes on a half-built station?"

"It's the way of construction. A well-fed worker is a happy worker. Our bunks might be small, but damn, do we eat well."

"I'll be back, and maybe you can snag one for me. Sorry about the order thing. It's what I'm used to. Put the machines in place and leave them in the netting, please. I shouldn't be too long. See you there, Finn." The private jetted away from the load, leaving it in the worker's large hands.

Cole followed the line on his HUD that took him up and around the top of the station. Chaz was guiding him to a half-built gantry. The private slowed as he approached. "I can't see anything that looks out of the ordinary," Cole reported.

"Inspector Sheila Mayer's EVA suit auto-reported a catastrophic failure in this location. She may have floated away from the station. Her geo-locator beacon is no longer transmitting."

Alant actively scanned the area for loose objects. In moments, the inside screen of his helmet populated with a combat tactical display highlighting the station and everything else within a kilometer. He dialed in on the gantry.

"Got you." A floating body tethered on the other side. He accelerated at maximum toward it, then cut the jets and executed a roll to point in the opposite direction so he could slow down. He drifted slightly past her, thinking he saw a movement. He hurried back to examine her suit. It had been slashed and shredded, but she had been wearing a shipsuit underneath. The private hugged her to him. He looked for the nearest airlock, catching sight of the Magistrate and her bodyguard as she exited.

He gestured for them to stay there and carefully headed that way, jerking to a halt when the tether caught. It sprang back, pulling the private and his precious cargo back toward the gantry. A metal fixture swung down, hit the private in the helmet, and continued scraping down his armored back.

The combat systems showed green across the board. Construction debris swinging free. An accident.

They floated toward the tether link. He grabbed the eyebolt with one hand and deftly unhooked the clasp, then kicked off the strut to propel himself back toward the airlock. The Magistrate was pointing at something over his head. He looked up in time to see the scythe-like device heading toward him a second time.

With a move accelerated by his mechanized armor, he turned to put the inspector on the opposite side away from the debris, caught the swinging arm, and twisted it off the gantry. He swiveled back and forth, looking for anything else that would keep him from getting the inspector inside the station.

Finding nothing, he continued to the airlock, where he deposited the inspector between the Magistrate and Lindy. He tried to hug the ceiling to give them enough room.

When the light turned green, Rivka pulled her hood back and bent down to examine the woman. Her suit had tried to seal itself, but the damage was too severe. However, it had indirectly sealed the inspector's shipsuit beneath. Because of that, Sheila had survived. When the door popped, the medical personnel were waiting.

Rivka thanked them and stepped aside so they could work on the victim. They left her in her suit to keep the wounds sealed, putting her on the gurney exactly as the private had delivered her and hurrying away.

The private held the metal scythe away from those not wearing armor. When it was just Alant, Rivka, and Lindy, the Magistrate took a closer look. "What the hell is this thing, and what happened out there?"

"Came out of nowhere, ma'am." He held it before her but wouldn't let her touch it. The edges were jagged, with separate quills like a feather. It looked like it was designed to shred an EVA suit and the person within.

"We'll see if anyone knows what this thing is or what purpose it could possibly serve on a space station." Rivka's lip curled in disgust. She glared at the metal, willing it to give up its secrets.

"Want me to put it in the hangar bay?"

Rivka nodded. "And stop by that gantry and get video of everything."

The private backed into the airlock, cycled it, and went

on his way around the other side of the station. Rivka looked around to find herself alone with Lindy.

"You wouldn't know the way back, would you?"

Lindy chuckled. "Not a chance."

Chaz, can you get us back to where we need to go?

I can try, Magistrate. The AI attempted to sound sincere.

And get the construction drawings for everything related to the gantry where the inspector was injured.

Rivka sat to the side and watched the inspectors. They shifted nervously within an environment that should have been comfortable but was exactly the opposite.

"Marks," the Magistrate said softly and pointed to a chair next to her. "Lindy, have everyone else wait in the corridor. Make sure they don't talk to each other."

Lindy nodded and ushered the group out, closing the door behind her as she left the Magistrate alone with the wrinkly, purple alien.

She laid her pad on the table between them and showed the structure with the pin and ram that had been responsible for the last death. She also showed the construction drawing where it was supposed to be a rigid connection. "Do you know who inspected this section?"

Don't ask a question you don't know the answer to. In this instance, Marks had signed off that the structure had been built in accordance with specifications.

He looked at the picture and then the drawing. He produced a pen-like device from his pocket, punched a button on it, and laid it next to the pad.

He breathed softly as he stared at the picture. "You know it was me," he admitted. "But that's not what I inspected. We get accused all the time, so most of us, if not all, carry our own video capture. Have your AI access my spy cam. I've unlocked it."

Rivka studied it without touching the device. "Those things are illegal."

He shrugged one shoulder. "Better that than getting accused of murder or getting hammered in a lawsuit for shoddy construction."

Rivka opened the comm channel through her datapad and put her AI on speaker. "Chaz, can you access the video device that's next to the pad? You should be getting an open signal."

"I see it. What images would you like to see?"

"The incident labeled 'Echo-5.' Marry the images from the pen with those of the construction drawing."

The datapad started to flash stills from the video capture. It stopped on an image that looked exactly like the construction drawing, a hard point sealed with a weld and two transverse struts.

They both leaned in to examine the image. "Date stamp on that?"

Chaz put the date and time of the image at the bottom, then arranged the two images side by side. Four days between the inspection data and the incident that had claimed the worker's life, and then seven more days before Rivka's picture.

Marks shook his head.

"Who approved the modification and rebuild of this joint?"

"There is no record of any modifications," Chaz replied.

Rivka relaxed into her chair, laced her fingers together, and stared into the distance. "We know that people are building stuff without the bots. Can they build something like this modification without technical assistance?"

"Humanity built spaceships without the aid of artificial intelligence or welding bots. Other races are equally adept at creation, even for the purpose of destruction."

Marks continued to look at the images on the datapad. "We inspect to the drawings. If someone makes changes after the inspection, we can't certify our work. We have to reinspect everything." He hung his head at the monumental amount of work before him. "We're going to need more people."

"No one is inspecting anything until we find out who is trying to kill the workers." Rivka tipped her head back and stared at the ceiling. "Chaz, get me Sheila's status, please. She may not know what happened, but I want her to live. I don't want anyone else to die while building a damn space station."

"Nor I, Magistrate," the inspector assured.

"Who can do this work without anyone else knowing?"

"That is the question I would love to know the answer to." Marks' sincerity radiated from him. Rivka could feel the strength of his emotion without having to touch him.

"What kind of ownership do the inspectors have of the station?"

It didn't take Marks long to spool up his response. "It's ours. We may not fit the plates or girders and seal the welds, but we are the last line of defense that the station is safe. It is our necks on the line if there's a failure."

"That wasn't the impression you gave me when you arrived earlier. You seemed almost indifferent to the fact that people were getting killed." Rivka watched the pupils of his eyes, his breathing, and a vein throbbing on the side of his wrinkled neck.

"We knew we had nothing to do with any of this. It wasn't indifference. We honestly thought the crew was being excessively careless. We're behind schedule, and the super is pushing hard, just like the administrator. Both those guys only see penalties for being late, not the penalty of faulty construction. They figure it'll be good enough since everything is over-engineered."

"It is, isn't it?" Rivka wondered.

"Three times greater than calculated maxes, so yes. It doesn't have to be perfect to be completely safe. I'm concerned about a cascade failure where one item creates extreme stress on a second part, compounding with each new failure." He tapped on the construction drawing thumbnail and it filled the datapad's screen. "With a pivot point here versus a hard connection, the engineering throughout the rest of this structure is changed. We need new calculations, tolerances, and construction specs."

Rivka nodded, watching the inspector instead of the screen. Chaz would take care of the technical details, backed up by Ankh and Erasmus. Those three would validate the engineering. Her focus was on the people involved. Nothing happened without an intervention.

Who was changing the construction?

"Chaz, I need every bit of footage from outside the station reviewed to confirm who worked in those areas between the moment this picture was taken and the time of the injury. Four days' worth. I know it was already reviewed in the safety investigation, but go through it yourself with fresh eyes."

"I shall run through it, although you'll have to forgive me in that I have no eyes. I submit that I can see quite well, though."

"My apologies, Chaz! I know you'll be thorough. While you're at it, if you could review the footage on the other four incidents…make that five. Give us a look at what happened where Sheila was inspecting for four days prior."

"I'll deliver my results the second I have them."

"I know you will, Chaz. You are eminently reliable and a valuable member of my crew."

Marks cocked a single heavy eyebrow with a few crazy hairs sticking out of it.

Rivka ignored him and continued with her line of thought. "Explain the process for taking a work package, getting the material, and then doing the work."

"We inspect the work once it's done. We're not involved with the other part of construction. You'll have to ask the construction superintendent for those details. I can describe our process," he offered.

Rivka nodded while building within her mind roles and responsibilities, the rules of the construction road. Every bit of information was important until it wasn't. She wouldn't know until later. In the interim, this was the time-consuming part of the investigation. She took a deep breath and ordered a drink and a snack from the food processor installed in the room.

"That's not functional yet," Marks told her after it didn't deliver anything.

"It's on," she countered, leaning to the side to avoid reflections, making sure the panel was lit.

"But the nutrition pack transfer system is not finished. Once that hookup takes place, the processors will come online."

The inspector knew what was operational.

Chaz, can you order some chow for me?

Before the AI could respond, the door opened and Red walked in, his head bent and his armor loose on his body. He still filled the doorway, but as a normally large man and not a shambling behemoth.

"There's the man I first met all those years ago!" Rivka declared and hurried to give Red a hug.

"I feel small and insignificant," he muttered.

Marks looked shocked, rocking back to see the big man's face.

"You aren't. You never were, and will never be small or insignificant. I might even say that you're the cat's ass. Focus on what you are and not what you aren't."

Red nodded, tight-lipped.

"Does Lindy still love you?" Rivka asked pointedly.

Red was taken aback. "Well, I think so."

"Goddamn men." Rivka grabbed Red by the arms and shook him. "Of course, she does. You deserve each other. Now that's the end of that. Don't make me kick your ass in training just to put you in your place."

"But you can't take me," Red replied, stretching upward and outward before deflating slightly.

"Damn straight, and don't forget it! Chow is coming, so order yourself something through Chaz."

Red pointed to the food processor.

"Doesn't work yet."

Once Rivka was back in her seat, she returned her attention to Marks. "Where were we?"

"Inspection processes. Sit back, this could take a while," the inspector warned.

CHAPTER EIGHT

Hangar Bay Aleph, Federation Border Station 13 – Under Construction

Private Cole hovered over the mass of welding machines. The metal scythe-like contraption lay off to the side. Finn loudly sipped his shake.

"You got one for me?" Cole asked.

"How can you drink it when you're wearing that thing?"

"I don't wear this all the time. I'll take it off when I return to *Wyatt*."

"That's what they all say," the construction worker quipped.

"I'm beginning to like you, which means when the shooting starts, I'll kill you last."

"What the fuck?" Finn was unused to military humor.

Cole had a good laugh at the man's expense. "You need to lighten up, Frances."

"How did you know my name was Frances? No one knows that!" He looked around quickly. "Shut it, dude! I need that to be kept secret."

Cole was confused but adhered to the philosophy that sometimes he didn't want to know. "It'll never pass my lips again. You keep your secret if you can. The Magistrate will know, I guarantee it. And if I understand the stories about her, she'll know why you want to keep it secret too. I hope it's nothing illegal for your sake."

Private Cole kept the volume low so his voice didn't project throughout the hangar bay even though they were the only ones there. Various bubbles on the ceiling suggested a myriad of cameras were watching them.

Magistrate, I have the welding machines and other hardware secure, Cole reported.

I'll be down in a few.

"A few" was relative. More than three hours passed before Rivka appeared. She looked tired, but the private perked up. He was still in his armor. He was ready to get out of it.

Red and Lindy strolled into the hangar bay first and checked the area, finding only Finn and Cole. Finn was sprawled on a large crate, sound asleep.

Ankh, help me understand what I'm looking at, Rivka requested.

Fine, the Crenellian replied. *Zoom in on the machines as you separate them.*

Ankh continued to give directions until most of the machines were disassembled.

They are manually-operated, automatic welding machines, nothing more. They don't have a computer interface of any sort.

I took them apart so you could tell me they don't apply? You knew that, didn't you?

You learned that these machines did not contribute to the construction anomalies. Those who operated them, on the other hand, could be involved, although I don't think so. A manual weld is different from a machine weld. The welds at Point Echo-5 were machine welds, but the winged spear-shaped object? Please bring that to the ship for further analysis.

It would have helped had you told me those things earlier, Rivka challenged the Crenellian. *You should have been here taking these apart, not me.*

Busy. Ankh signed off after his claim.

"That bastard," Rivka grumbled. "You can have your machines back, Finn." Cole stomped over and woke him up to tell him that he was free to go once he acquired a chocolate shake for the private.

And the Magistrate.

Onboard *Wyatt Earp*, Federation Border Station 13 – Under Construction

"These people love their jobs," Rivka droned before sipping her shake and smiling. "If I can judge by the number of words they used to describe them."

"Isn't that a good thing?" Jay asked. She held one end of a small rope, and Floyd was tugging on the other. Wenceslaus had figured out how to climb the wall and was perched on a decorative shelf overlooking the room through slitted eyes. He had his front paws tucked underneath his chest, showing no inclination of moving.

"It's better than if they said nothing. They were forthcoming with information. An endless amount of information, but not much of it was useful. Still, weeding through information to find the applicable details is in a barrister's job description."

Jay nodded, glancing surreptitiously at the chocolate shake. Rivka handed it over with a warning. "Don't drink too fast. It'll freeze your brain."

The young woman tucked the hair on one side of her head behind her ear and took a careful sip. She'd had one before, but every shake was a new experience. "I need Ankh to program these into our food processor."

"I will be forever in your debt if you can accomplish that feat."

Me, me! the wombat cried. Jay took the lid off the cup and held it down. Rivka sighed. She had entertained thoughts of getting another drink, but those hopes were crushed as she watched Floyd stuff her big snout into the remainder of the ice cream. *More!*

"No more," Jay told the wombat and gave her a hearty ear scratch.

"I'm with you, sister. We need more. You work on Ankh. I have an endless amount of chaff to wade through to hopefully find a couple kernels of wheat."

The Magistrate retired to her luxury stateroom, breathing deeply of a scent she couldn't recognize but suspected was an essential oil Jay had brought aboard to help fight the Skaine stench. Rivka wasn't sure the odor had not permeated even the metal of the ship. Jay was engaged in a life-and-death struggle to minimize the assault on the olfactory glands of the crew.

"There you are." On the counter next to her small

kitchen, Rivka eyed a tiny bottle with brown sticks diffusing scent into the air. She inhaled deeply, enjoying the mix of fragrances. "Kudos to you, Jay and thank you. Chaz, remind me to do something for Jay when we get back home."

"I think you are home, Magistrate," the AI replied.

"Don't be creepy, Chaz. This is our home away from home. Maybe we can refer to Station 7 as our second home."

"I will remind you, Magistrate. On a different note, I am ready with my conclusions of the video analysis."

"Pray tell, Chaz. My guess is that no one went anywhere near the area in question."

"I would like to tell you that is the case, but I can't," Chaz replied.

Rivka's ears perked up. "We have a suspect!" she declared.

"I can't tell you that either, Magistrate. You see, the official feeds have been doctored. The video of Echo-5 is fake."

"Isn't that interesting?" Rivka commented before taking a seat and contemplating its meaning and her next steps. "We need to find who had access to Bluto, to the storage, and to the physical video setup."

"I've begun digging into the source of the changes to the official video."

"Thanks, Chaz. You haven't found anything yet?"

"Nothing yet, Magistrate."

"Get help from Ankh and Erasmus if you need it."

The slight crackle over the speakers disappeared, suggesting Chaz had left the conversation. Rivka took a seat on her couch and kicked back. She brought up the large screen and started scrolling through the mind-numbing transcripts from her interviews with the inspectors. She'd have to do the same thing with the workforce, too. Every single worker who was assigned to that area.

Had they seen anything? Probably not. There were five hundred workers putting the station together. Only five hundred. It was a manageable number, but it would still be time-consuming. She had spent hours with the inspectors, but they had signed off on the work. They were the last to see it before it was modified.

How could someone make major structural modifications without being seen?

"Chaz, get me Bluto, please, and stay on the line to double-check things if needed."

"Of course," Chaz replied. A click signaled when an additional comm line opened.

"This is Bluto," the station EI said.

"Bluto, Magistrate Rivka Anoa. Do you know why I'm here?"

"You are investigating construction accidents."

"That's correct. Do you know anything about the construction modifications at sites Echo-5, Delta-4, and Charlie-3?"

"I'm sure I don't know."

"That's not a very EI-like answer." Rivka sucked her lip as she looked at the screen showing an interview transcript. It filled in her words as she spoke.

"It's the only EI answer I have. 'I think I don't know' would give me more credit than I deserve for my ability to generate independent thoughts more akin to a sentient being's. I am sure I don't know is the best and only answer I have," Bluto countered.

"Who modified the videos?" Rivka asked, impatient with the EI's extended explanation.

"I'm sure I don't know."

Rivka took a deep breath and waited. An EI. Programmed responses only. There was no reason to be upset. It didn't have the capacity for sarcasm.

It sounded like it, though. *I'm sure I don't know.*

Rivka changed tack to something the EI could answer. "What is your process for recording and storing the video from the camera providing oversight of the area marked Echo-5?"

Bluto explained the capture parameters and pathways of the digital delivery and the exact location within the new organic storage system where it would wait until retrieved.

"There has to be a record of each time the video is accessed."

"There is," Bluto agreed.

"Great. Who accessed it and when?"

"Boran Waldin three hours after the safety incident, and then Chaz two hours ago."

"Did either of those two modify the file?"

"No."

"Somebody did. Who else accessed the file?" Rivka was growing impatient again.

"I'm sure I don't know."

Rivka thought her head was going to explode. She stood and returned to the counter where the diffuser passively spread a pleasant scent through her stateroom. She breathed in the smell. Lilacs—something Rivka had never touched in real life. She imagined them as purple with dashes of red in a stately flower that towered majestically over the others within the garden. Wyatt Earp had a small hydroponics bay. Maybe she'd plant flowers if Jay hadn't already.

"Chaz, I'd like a private side-bar with you, please."

"We are now secure. Bluto is standing by."

"We need to look into Bluto's programming. Someone is able to bypass his normal command and control circuitry. It is unfathomable that he couldn't tell who accessed his secure files."

"I believe it is fathomable. Ankh was into his system in moments after making the attempt. I doubt Bluto knew his circuits were open to the universe even though Ankh said the EI was forthcoming, I expect that related to the security of access and not that Bluto was aware."

"Is he that limited in scope? Is he correct when he says he doesn't know?"

"I suspect he does know but isn't able to analyze the limitations to dig deeper into the anomalies. He checks the standard file coding, and it tells him it is unmolested when we know that it has been changed. He accepts the file properties as absolute truth and is unable to look at them from any other angle."

"I'll buy that. So how do we dig deeper into his system and look for what he can't?"

"We're already doing that, Magistrate. I initiated the search immediately following his last denial of knowledge. I refuse to let a fellow software system self-destruct under questioning."

Rivka opened her mouth to reply but couldn't come up with the words. She settled on something simple. "Let me know when you have something. I'll be touring the ship."

She left the comfort of her stateroom behind and headed straight for the engine room. She hadn't been in the area before and was surprised by its spaciousness. She wondered how much of the ship it entailed. She hadn't bothered with digging into the size of her ship, but it was much larger than Grainger's frigate, so much so that she wondered if they were the same class. She wasn't sure what was the next size up from a frigate. Maybe his was a large corvette and not a frigate at all.

Did it matter?

Yes, she decided. Words were important because they created the common frame of reference that made all conversations possible and gave negotiations a chance for success. A mutual understanding was important for language as a whole. To communicate a concept, one must use words with agreed-upon definitions.

She would check later into the various ship classes.

Rivka walked through the space with her hands clasped behind her back as if conducting an inspection. Clodagh was elbow-deep in a panel, and a small toolkit sat on a stand beside her.

"Magistrate! Welcome to my nightmare."

The greeting caught Rivka off-guard. She was still thinking through her conversation with Bluto. "It's not that bad, is it?"

"Just a figure of speech, Magistrate. *Wyatt* is a great ship." Clodagh wiped her hands on a rag even though they looked clean, and afterward, the rag looked clean, too. "It's old enough to need some tender loving care while new enough that nothing major is going to go wrong, plus, the little guy has upgraded some of the system buses and energy conduits. If we used all the power available to us, it could either propel us across multiple galaxies at one pop or reduce us to trillions of molecules accelerated to near-light speed, expanding like a supernova."

Rivka chuckled. "No in-between, huh?"

"It's all or nothing, do or die." Clodagh nodded emphatically. "Can I help you with something?"

"Looking for Ankh."

The lieutenant pointed with her chin. Rivka winked and walked in that direction. She found the Crenellian huddled within a holo-field.

"Ankh," she said loud enough that there was no doubt he could hear her. She counted to five before sticking her hand through the three-dimensional projection and waving before his face. He didn't respond, just kept tapping on the holographic touchpoints.

She poked him in the chest. When he didn't respond to that, she poked him a second time in the forehead. Finally, the holoscreens dropped. He turned his unemotional eyes to her. "Humans have to be the most impatient of species. First, Terry Henry Walton, and now you. Can you not wait until I'm done?" He asked evenly, emotionlessly without moving his head or engaging in any other way.

"But you're never done, Ankh. You always have something. You and Ted are the busiest people I have ever met. You don't waste a single moment. I feel like I am always bothering you. I want to hurry up and be done with it so you can get back to what you're doing. I apologize now and forever because I suspect that I will always interrupt you."

At least in your mind, she thought.

"I will accept your premise that I am always busy, like now. I'm busy. What do you want, and how much time will it take?"

"We need to speak in complete privacy, with no one, not Erasmus or Chaz or anyone else listening. I need answers only you can provide."

"Fine, although Erasmus can't be silenced. He sees and hears everything I do. If you want to talk to me, you talk to him, too. We'll keep your secret, Magistrate." Ankh didn't sound convincing. The emotionless tone of his small voice was usually unpersuasive, but the words? Those carried the full weight of his message.

"I agree," the Magistrate replied. Ankh closed his eyes for a moment. The hairs on Rivka's arm stood up as something unidentifiable passed over her.

Ankh opened his eyes and informed her that she could speak freely.

"What did you do?"

"EM field. Is that what you wanted to talk to me about?"

She knew he was being sarcastic, but his point was clear. She needed to get to her question. "How can we tell if Bluto has been compromised, or Chaz for that matter?"

"If anyone is accessing a system from the outside, they will leave telltale signs. It's not hard to find them if you know what you're looking for."

"You assured me you could get into systems without leaving fingerprints." Rivka hovered her hand near the

Crenellian, not quite zombie pose, but close enough for it to draw Ankh's attention. He watched her hand as he answered.

"I'm not just anyone. I could tell if someone got into a system even if they had authorization."

"Can you check Bluto first, and then Chaz, without anyone knowing, of course."

"Of course," Ankh repeated. "Why did you have to ask this in private?"

"I think our perp knows everything that Bluto knows. They might have gotten into Chaz, too. A standard interrogation technique is to separate the witnesses and have them give their version of events. Then we bounce the different statements against each other to see what's different. I've asked Bluto questions, but I felt he purposely avoided giving a direct answer. I'm not sure he answered any of my questions, come to think about it. And if the perp knows where we're looking, he may be good enough to drop red herrings across his tracks."

"I'll take a look. Is that all?"

"It is. Thank you, Ankh. You are a valuable member of the crew."

Ankh shooed her away, and as soon as she was outside his bubble, the holo-screens returned. The Crenellian disappeared within the confines of his own digital construct, tapping and spinning as part of his interface dance.

Rivka didn't know if positive reinforcement worked on the Crenellian, but she was a believer. Anyone who helped needed to know they were helpful. Even if she had to play twenty questions to get there. She could skip the small talk with Ankh, and that was the revelation she needed.

Get to it and save valuable time for both of them.

She nodded to Clodagh as she passed, but the engineer didn't notice. She remained focused on the panel and her detail work within.

Once in the main section of her ship, she stopped and took in the space. The airlock, the long corridor to the bridge, a transverse corridor to take her to the port side of the ship. So much space. Aurora popped into the corridor from a side room, waved, and continued toward the bridge.

I have to spend more time with the crew, Rivka vowed. *But first, I have a murderer to catch.*

"Red! Lindy!" she bellowed down the corridor, stalking forward confidently

"I thought I heard a bistok in heat," Red quipped when he stuck his head into the corridor. "Was that you?"

"I shall make small jokes for the rest of your existence." The look on Red's face suggested such jibes wouldn't be well-received. "Okay, I won't. Lindy, are you in there?"

"I don't have my clothes on," she called from within. Rivka stopped instantly and turned away.

"I don't want to know. We need to head back into the station. I want to talk with some more people and see some of the interfaces that have already been installed."

Red smiled mischievously as he blocked the door with his body. Rivka held out her hand, and he shook it warmly.

"Welcome back, big man. We missed you, but never again. I need you with me. Get in there and get ready. Full gear." Rivka took two steps before stopping and turning back. "Those aren't your quarters."

He laughed in reply.

It dawned on the Magistrate. "Oh no, you don't. You are not going to 'break in' every space on this ship, do you hear me, Vered?"

Red tried to look contrite.

"What's the bet?" Rivka asked.

"A date for the wedding," Lindy added, adjusting her top as she leaned past Red.

"I'm the captain of the ship as well as a Magistrate. I can marry you guys here or in space. Why don't we just get it over with so I don't have to wonder when you've been in my quarters?"

"That will be the toughest…" Red said slowly.

"Come on, you sickeningly sweet lovebirds. Let's go find someone's ass that needs kicking."

"My vote is for that weasely workforce administrator, Fleener." Lindy made like she wanted to spit from the distaste of having said his name.

"Give us five, Magistrate. We'll be there, dressed for war."

"We still haven't drawn blood, but it's been less than a full day so far. The money was on two; we'll see if we can make it none."

"If you catch a guy who has killed five people and tried to murder a sixth, I doubt you'll leave him intact," Red offered before heading for his quarters.

"Serial killer," Rivka said softly. "And you're right. There's no room in this universe for anyone who enjoys killing people."

CHAPTER NINE

Federation Border Station 13 – Under Construction

Would she find him over the course of another day? The odds suggested she would. Rivka had no idea what went into the calculations, but with Ankh making them, they'd been accurate more often than not. Free will was eminently predictable if one included the right variables.

The Magistrate wouldn't ask. Listening to Ankh lecture on math would be as exciting as watching water evaporate.

Rivka returned to her stateroom to don ballistic protection over her shipsuit. She wanted people to talk, and they didn't when she was dressed more formally, even if it was only in a jumpsuit. It looked civilian. With her armor and shipsuit, she looked military.

With a final discriminating review of her appearance, Rivka tucked Reaper into her Magistrate's jacket pocket along with her datapad and headed for the exit. She found Red and Lindy waiting for her. Jay was standing nearby.

"Can I go, too?" she asked.

"We're going to high-stress some of the suspects. I'm not sure you want to be there for that," Rivka advised.

"You have suspects?" Jay seemed pleasantly surprised.

"A few over five hundred. I'll whittle them down, starting in about five minutes."

Jay frowned and dug at the deck with her toe.

"What's your offer?" Rivka asked.

"I'll watch and engage with those who are waiting their turn to be high-stressed, as you called it."

"It's a technique to get the suspect to make a mistake because he's emotionally charged. Disengage the thinking brain. Engage the fight-or-flight mode."

"I can help with those waiting or afterward."

"Afterward?"

"Somebody has to soothe frayed nerves and calm the masses. We don't want enemies, do we?"

"You are correct, Jay. Please join us."

Floyd bounced up to Jay and vibrated with anticipation at leaving the ship.

"Please?" Jay asked.

"Any illusions that I'm in charge have been utterly shattered." The Magistrate looked down at her outfit and then at Jay and Floyd.

"So much for coming across as a hardass."

Red pointed to himself and Lindy. "We got your back, Magistrate."

They looked the part. Both carried railguns across chests covered by the ballistic armor that stretched over most of their bodies. They wore helmets, too, chin straps in place to keep them tight should the bodyguards have to fire and maneuver.

"If we need to intimidate anyone, I have you two." Rivka walked through the open airlock into the extended corridor that locked tightly to her ship. At the end of the gantry, Boran waited.

Safety Manager Boran Waldin looked like he'd had better days.

"When's the last time you slept?" Rivka asked, resting her hand on his shoulder as he slumped against the wall. His mind told her nothing except that he was physically and emotionally exhausted. The feeling of failure was pervasive.

"At least Sheila looks like she's going to pull through," Rivka added when Boran didn't speak. He nodded.

Rivka continued, "You could not have prevented any of this. There's no safety policy or training in the known universe that was going to keep workers from getting killed. We don't just have a murderer; we have a serial killer. Do you know what makes a serial killer different?"

Boran took note of the new conversation. He shook his head, looking up to meet Rivka's gaze.

"No remorse. They get a thrill from the kill without any downside. They don't feel guilt. Let me reiterate. The murderer was going to kill people no matter what you did. You had no chance. Make no mistake—we will find this person, human or alien. They are going against me, and they will not win."

When he finally realized Rivka wasn't alone, he perked up.

He took in the group, giving Red and Lindy as hard a look as he could manage. When he saw Jay behind them, he stopped and stared.

"You're back. I was lost but now I'm found. You're gorgeous!" he blurted before slapping a hand over his mouth and looking wide-eyed at the Magistrate. "I mean, where do you want to go?"

Floyd giggled and waddled through the entourage to give Boran a good sniff.

"No animals in an active construction zone," he said without thinking.

Rivka smirked. "I thought I ordered all construction halted?"

"You did. There is no active construction zone. I'm sorry. I got all confused when I saw Aphrodite appear before me."

Rivka couldn't help but laugh. "That's one way. She's a wombat and her name is Floyd, but if you want to call her Aphrodite, I'm sure she'll be good with it."

"That's not…"

Rivka stopped him. "Take us to the workforce lounge. We're going to line up the workers and talk to them one after another, daisy-chain style."

The safety manager looked back and forth between Jay and Rivka. Jay twirled her hair around one finger while returning Boran's look. Red stepped in front of her to block their view of each other and gestured for Boran to lead the way.

Rivka pointed.

"The worker lounge. There's some good food up there. I think they're throwing a party."

"A party?" the Magistrate wondered.

Boran started walking, furtively glancing over his

shoulder to catch glimpses of Jay, who was now carrying Floyd because the wombat was already tired.

"It's a morale booster, the super said, but I doubt it'll work. The guys want to get paid. No pay, no morale."

"Then all the better that I get to talk with everyone. It's nice that we have most of them, if not all, in one place."

"I doubt more than half are at the party."

"When I show up, they should feel festive because once we have the perpetrator or perps in hand, everyone can get back to work. We all want the same thing. It's important these people understand that."

Boran nodded heartily. "I've explained until I'm blue in the face. They don't see the forest for the trees."

They continued in silence until they reached the elevator. The Magistrate was skeptical about entering.

Red walked in and started inspecting it. He removed one of Ankh's surveillance devices from his pocket, and his lips moved as he spoke to the Crenellian using the comm chip. Lindy blocked the door with her body while Red thoroughly examined their ride.

"I don't see anything, and Ankh says there are no extraneous signals."

Rivka tried to be nonchalant about it but still found her legs heavy with each step to board the elevator. Jay casually strolled aboard, brushing heavily against the safety manager on her way in. Floyd left a clump of hair on his coveralls.

"Time to go," Rivka said. Red stared at Boran until he looked away. He punched the button for the fourth deck from the top and away they went. Rivka was as stiff as an I-beam until the door opened. She hurried out before any of the others despite Red trying to stop her. Lindy rushed to get in front.

"What's their hurry?" Boran asked.

"No one wants to get trapped in an elevator with Red. You know the rule: smallest person gets eaten first."

Boran leaned back and studied Jay's face.

"Are you serious?" Her expression gave nothing away. He declared, "You are *not* serious."

"As long as the elevator delivers us where we're supposed to go, you'll never have to find out."

"A mind like a steel trap. You are scintillating."

Someone cleared their throat. Rivka and her party were staring at the safety manager, along with the workers who were milling about in the corridor outside the massive break room. It had been reserved for their use as a recreation area during construction.

"The Great Waldini is trying to get a girlfriend!" someone called.

"Is that what that was? By the moons of Polaris, why isn't she running for her life?" another replied.

Rivka raised her hands for silence. "I need everyone to join me in the recreation room, please."

"Fuck off!" The muffled cry came from a tightly-packed group. Boran stormed into them, grabbed a short, round alien, and dragged him into the open.

"Apologize you twat!" Boran shook him.

"Sorry," the creature mumbled.

"Get your bowling-ball ass into the room like the Magistrate told you. The more you dick around out here, the longer you'll go without a paycheck. Help her solve these murders, you fucks!"

"So there is a brash side to you. Using it sparingly, too, I see. That's good. When you unleash it, they know you're serious." Rivka gestured for him to precede her into the room, but Red was already through the door with the last of those who had been standing in the corridor. Lindy waited. She'd go in last.

Rivka and Boran walked through the door together, to find Workforce Administrator Ossuary Fleener waiting with arms crossed.

"Good!" Rivka claimed. "You're here. Line everyone up. First person here, and then a single line that can snake around the rec area. I'll walk through and ask questions as I need."

Fleener didn't move.

"Lindy, throw him out. I'll conduct the interviews without him."

"It's my right to be here!" he stated as forcefully as he could muster.

"Are you their lawyer?" the Magistrate asked.

He sputtered before shaking his head. He held his ground, standing as tall as he was able.

"Mr. Fleener. If this were a civil matter, your participation would be called for, but since this is a criminal matter, you have no right to represent these workers. This is the second time you've tried to interfere with my investigation. I accuse you of criminal obstruction, and since the crime that you are interfering with is murder, obstruction is a felony commensurate with aiding and abetting. I find you guilty. You'll be incarcerated in the station brig…"

"It's not built yet," Boran whispered.

"You'll be confined to quarters," Rivka corrected with a

curt nod. She spied two Yollins standing in a shadow against the wall. "Hey! Are you the super's security detail?"

One Yollin walked forward and clicked his mandibles. "We are."

"Take him to his quarters and secure him there." She turned back to Fleener, who stood with his mouth open as if caught mid-scream. "If I see you set one foot out of your room, I will send you to Jhiordaan for the rest of your miserable life. You have fucked with me for the last time."

The crowd separated, creating a wide path for the large, carapaced creatures. They strolled through, grabbed the workforce administrator without breaking stride, and dragged him ass-backwards through the door. Once out of sight, he started to scream. Rivka waved at Lindy to secure the room.

She closed the door, which cut off the noise.

"I need you single-file. First person right here." She physically moved a wrinkly purple worker into place. The others fell in behind, and soon, the line snaked back and forth throughout the room. Lindy positioned herself near the door, watching the crowd. Jay strolled about, drawing the eyes of many workers. Boran hovered protectively.

"Have you never seen a woman before?" Rivka muttered.

Boran stepped toward the Magistrate. "Construction life, ma'am. We don't see a whole lot of civilians in our line of work. Ever. We go from job to job. Many of these people have families but don't see them much."

"What kind of life is that?" Rivka asked, trying to keep her voice low. She wished she had thought to ask more background questions earlier instead of in front of the nervous workforce.

"We like to build things. Have you ever seen something take shape through the power of your own hands? It's the thrill of the process, problem-solving, attention to detail, and the gratification of the final product."

"Compelling. It takes a rare type, which means the right workers are probably hard to find."

"Which means the pay is good," Boran finished her thought.

"When we're working," someone mumbled from nearby.

"Then let's get to it." Rivka approached the first in line. He stiffened. "There's no reason to be concerned as long as you're not involved. You're not, are you?"

She put out her hand and touched their arms as she walked past while looking from face to face.

Gambling.

Drinking.

Cutting a corner on a fit-up.

She stopped and pulled the alien female from the line. Rivka turned to Boran. "You'll need to double-check this one's work. She's been cutting corners."

The safety manager's surprise was mirrored by the look on the humanoid's wide face. He took down her name and made her sit in a corner. Rivka grimaced at the public excoriation. She imagined the worker wearing a dunce cap.

Shouldn't have taken shortcuts, Rivka thought and dismissed her from her mind.

"As long as you're not involved, there's nothing to worry about," the Magistrate reiterated to get their minds churning before she continued seeing their thoughts. The workers were close together, and many of the thoughts were jumbled, but Rivka knew what she was looking for—someone trying to hide their after-hours work to set up the killing traps.

Boran had been right about the presence of civilians. Jay, Lindy, and even the Magistrate were in the thoughts of too many.

Most tried to hide their attraction, but it was too strong. No serial killers. Too many off-color jokes told in the shadows.

If that was what a worker was worried about, the station was in good hands.

Petty thievery. Rivka stopped.

"I'm going to need to see your locker," she told the crusty old worker. He might have been human. She couldn't be certain.

"Why?" he demanded, instantly defensive, anxious, and afraid.

Rivka didn't have time to play games. "Because you've been stealing from your co-workers. Turn out your pockets."

He tried to give her the finger, but before his hand was chest-high, Red had grabbed him and twisted his arm behind his back. The bodyguard wrapped the man's free arm up and pulled tight enough that he started to gasp for breath. Rivka dug her fingers into his pocket. He made the mistake of trying to kick her. She kneed him in the groin, driving his head upward until it impacted with Red's chin.

"Enough games, fucker," Red growled, picking the man up and slamming him face-first onto the deck.

"I knew something wasn't right about that asshole!" someone called, and the workers piled on with declarations of how much they hated the man.

Rivka held up the ring she had pulled from the man's pocket. "Looks like a wedding ring." The inscription was alien but translated to BS+BJ. She steeled her expression at the unfortunate initials. "BS?"

"Hey!" A tall and gangly alien who could have been related to the Keome stepped forward and tried to kick the man on the ground. Rivka stepped in front of him before he got close enough. "Yeah, that's mine."

He spat toward the man, nearly hitting Red. The big man turned his face toward the alien with an expression that said he better go away unless he wanted a severe beatdown.

"Sorry," the tall alien grumbled before getting back in line, all the while holding his ring to his chest.

Rivka stepped back to take it all in. Everyone had their secrets, upon which she was intruding. Some of them, like the stolen property, needed to be public, but the private thoughts of naked females, herself included, were things none of them were sharing openly. Thoughts rarely became actions, Rivka had found.

She wasn't looking for those who had not yet committed a crime, but those who already had. Six times trying to kill a worker, five times succeeding. The violence of murder left an indelible mark on one's brain.

She carried her own scars from homicides, from executions, from battles.

Red zip-tied the thief and shoved him into the corner

next to the female. He turned to face away from his fellows.

"Let's get this done," the Magistrate declared. "Which one of you is comfortable with the murder of your co-workers?"

A harsh question, but it would get their emotions churning. She hurried through the crowd. More thoughts of respect and gratitude. A barracks thief was the lowest of the low, stealing from friends. They were glad to have that resolved. They were glad someone like Rivka was on the job, accepting no bullshit. She finished her tour without finding anyone else who needed to be separated from the others.

She made a rough count. No more than a hundred and fifty. She was missing the majority.

"I need everyone here accounted for both manually and remotely. Have Bluto reconcile if he's capable, and I need you, Boran, to check these people off using a physical roster."

The safety manager moved to one of the food processors and used his management code to access its other three-dimensional printing functions. Within a minute, he had a complete printout of everyone and a pen to check them off. He sighed at the amount of work it would take, but no one was going anywhere until they were done.

"Let me know when you're done, and we'll cut these people loose. I will have to check one hundred percent of the workforce. Every single one of them."

Boran nodded as he went down the line, checking names off.

Rivka accessed a terminal near the door to the corridor

the workers were passing through once Boran had checked them off. She verified that Bluto was keeping track too, as a redundancy. Bluto was already finished.

The Magistrate wanted to use the mystique of her technique to create fear within her perp. He wasn't in this group, but he was somewhere and would be watching. And when Rivka approached, he'd start running. But he wasn't going to outrun Jay, or outfight Red or Lindy, or out-wile the Magistrate.

Ankh, do you have anything? she asked privately.

Can you be more specific?

The Magistrate snorted. Ankh gave her a certain stability she appreciated. *Has Bluto been compromised?*

An open question, to be sure. Bluto is not an EI. He has evolved. Bluto is an Artificial Intelligence with significant untapped potential since they treat him as an EI.

But he tells everyone he's an EI, Rivka countered, her fingers paused over the workstation's input device.

Regardless, it will take more time to dig deeper into his programming without his awareness. I will say that it is like what you do, but without the physical touching.

Only with digital fingers. Thanks, Ankh. Rivka looked blankly at the screen before her. Bluto had reported and was waiting patiently. An AI masquerading as an EI? She'd heard of that before. Who is the best judge of awareness? There was no magical line to step across. Ankh had spoken confidently. He'd left no doubt as to Bluto's status.

But why?

She shook her head to clear it. She was still searching for a serial killer. She found the construction superintendent standing behind her.

"You seemed lost in thought," he said. "Next time you rally the workforce or arrest one of my people, could you let me know?"

She straightened, and her eyes narrowed as she stared him down. He looked away.

"Please?"

"I'm conducting a criminal investigation that you delayed, which has cost us valuable evidence from the first two, and possibly the third incident as well. Negligence comes at a high cost. We're scrubbing your records, Mr. Orbal. If there's evidence that you tried to cover anything up, you'll be joining Mr. Fleener in his cell. Do you understand me?"

Rivka didn't know why she'd gotten angry so quickly at the super. She tried to analyze her emotions, but couldn't see past the administrator's interference. She was painting the super with that brush.

"I am sorry, Magistrate. I didn't mean to interfere with your investigation."

Rivka's lip twitched into a snarl. "They're not working until I'm finished, so you don't need to know what I'm doing. Return to your ship and stay there until I call for you." He looked at the floor as he stepped toward the door. "No. Wait. Get me the other three hundred and fifty workers. Bring them up here in groups of one hundred. I want every single worker both on the station or any of the supporting ships. Will that satisfy your need to know what's going on?"

"I didn't mean it that way." He looked more defensive than contrite.

"You're the construction superintendent, which means

you're used to being in charge and knowing everything that's going on. You let a serial killer have his way five times before you raised a red flag. That doesn't reflect well on you, Mr. Orbal. I appreciate you finally calling in the Federation. As much as you want to believe it, you were never in control, and you still aren't. Don't bluster around me ever again. Get those damn people up here right fucking now."

The super hurried away without replying. There was nothing for him to say. Steam boiled from Rivka's ears. At least she thought it did.

Jay sidled up beside her and talked out the side of her mouth. "What did he do to piss you off?"

"He tried to get in my business when I'm trying to catch a murderer."

"And you don't think you'll find him in the workforce," Jay added. She cradled a soundly sleeping wombat in her arms.

Rivka tipped her head back as she contemplated the words. Was she afraid she wouldn't find the perp? "Maybe that's it," she admitted. *What do I do if that's it?*

She didn't know, and that grated on her soul.

Federation Border Station 13 – Under Construction

"I'm going to beat his ass," Rivka growled.

The super cowered in the corner.

"He appears to be doing everything he can to avoid such a confrontation," Jay counseled.

Rivka tried to relax but couldn't. They were down to the last fifty names. The first four-hundred and fifty were searching the station and slowly bringing them to the recreation room. Bluto was assisting by directing workers to various locations he'd seen them transit.

The Magistrate crooked her finger at Red and Lindy. The two joined her and Jay. "Do you think he's running?"

"Running where?" Red asked. "According to Chaz, no one has left the station since we arrived, although space includes the super's ship. We need to thoroughly search it."

"Have Chaz scan the ship and see how many bodies are on board."

Lindy stared at a spot on the wall while she communicated with the AI.

"Zack, can I speak with you for a moment?" Rivka asked pleasantly. Red stepped up in case he needed to insert his body between the two. He hadn't seen Rivka act this hostile to someone who wasn't an obvious criminal, but he didn't know what she'd seen in the man's mind.

He didn't question her, but he would rather tangle with someone than let the Magistrate do it in front of everyone.

Take one for the team, he thought.

"How many people are on your ship?"

"Right now, that would be seventeen. It's twenty-one when my security team and I are on board," he replied, keeping his answer concise and to the point.

"I'll need to talk to them. Make sure they stay there, and bring your Yollins and the Ixtali up here with the final batch of workers."

"They are working to find the last few holdouts…"

Rivka's glare stopped him.

"I'll get them here immediately." He couldn't get away from her fast enough.

"I think you made him pee himself," Red whispered.

The Magistrate cocked one eyebrow before turning back to her datapad. She'd dispensed with the station's console. It didn't have everything she was looking for. It was easier to use her own device and get the supplemental information from Chaz, who was tapped into Bluto.

She selected the listing Bluto had been updating. "How many now?" she asked Boran. He snapped awake and started counting.

"Fifty-one."

"Does that include those on the super's ship?"

"It does not," the safety manager answered. "Then seventy-two. No, wait. You've already talked to the super. Seventy-one."

"Do you have them listed separately?"

He shook his head.

"Pull a separate list for the admin ship, please."

Boran gritted his teeth, unhappy about missing the obvious.

"When's the last time you slept?"

"About the third death," Boran deadpanned. "Or more recently, since well before you got here. When's the last time you slept, Magistrate?"

She furrowed her brow in thought. "I have not slept in the bed on my ship, so I guess it would have been back on Station 7. To answer your question, a while ago, but my team and I have special traits where we don't need as much sleep."

Floyd snuffled and adjusted in Jay's arms without waking up.

"Some of us don't have the special traits."

Jay giggled. "I know we can't wrap it up before we get the last of the workforce in here, but soon," Jay said in a soothing voice.

Rivka yawned, and it started a cascade. Red violently pinched his arm to avoid succumbing. He smiled, close-lipped when the feeling passed. Lindy shook her head.

"We're all tired…"

"He's running!" the construction superintendent yelled from across the room. "Right there." He pointed to a screen that no one could see. "A construction capsule for short flights. He's detached from the station and is heading toward deep space!"

The superintendent's voice rose with his final statement. He looked both triumphant and terrified.

Rivka closed her eyes. *Chaz, undock from the gantry and go get that capsule. Private Cole, get your suit on, and once the capsule is on board, secure it and the individual within. Bring them to the gantry, and we'll meet you there.*

Securing the airlock and undocking. We'll be back shortly, Chaz promised.

"Zack, please bring up the external cameras, and while we're watching *Wyatt Earp* catch the bad guy, you can tell me about who we'll find on board that construction capsule." Rivka walked across the room but stopped when the super projected the chase onto the big screen.

"The individual in question is Regina Novus, one of the Furlorian race, a new addition to the Federation. The Furlorians are a feline species, fierce individuals. There are very few of them left. She landed with us because of her flexibility and eye for detail. She can crawl through the tightest conduit. It's the craziest thing. She never did anything that would have raised any suspicion." The super pulled up her employment record. Standard entries. No flags for poor quality. No complaints from co-workers. No corrective actions.

"Where was she assigned in the days before each incident?"

The super thought for a moment, then switched to voice command and asked Bluto to show the information on a detailed drawing of the station. She had been in the area of each.

"What does Boran's location look like during the same timeframes?" Rivka asked.

Boran perked up and materialized next to the Magistrate. "I didn't do it!" He didn't know her game.

The map showed that Boran had been in those areas as well.

"But...but..." he stammered.

"Relax. I wanted to show that her proximity to the incidents is more typical than not. There's no proof that it was her, but this is how we build a case. If enough facts add up regarding motive, means, and opportunity, then we can tighten the thumbscrews."

"You use thumbscrews?" The super was incredulous.

"Figure of speech," Rivka shot back. "Regina Novus. I look forward to talking to you."

A group of workers walked through the door. The super waved them off. "You're not needed now."

"Stop!" Rivka demanded. "I still need to talk with every swinging dick on this station. What kind of investigation do you think I'm conducting? I talked to eighty percent of the workers and was satisfied? That doesn't fly in my book. One hundred percent. Every single person here."

The super threw his hands up in surrender. "Over here, please. Line up." He counted heads, and Boran marked off names.

"What do you know about the deaths of your co-workers?" she asked before strolling purposefully down the line, dragging her hand along their arms as she passed.

Confusion. Heard about it in the safety stand-down. Was sleeping when it happened. Damn, that green-haired chick is hot.

Rivka rubbed her temples. "They can go."

Red poked a thumb toward the door. "Away you go," he told them.

"Do we get paid for that? Should be an hour's worth," one of them complained.

Thirty-eight left. Thirty-seven since the pilot of the capsule looked to be in custody. The chase had lasted only a few seconds. The capsule and its pilot had been quickly captured and brought into the small hangar bay of Rivka's frigate. She expected Alant Cole had secured the pilot and was already taking her to the airlock for when the ship docked.

"Get me the last people. Have them waiting here when I return, unless I call you, and then bring them to my interview room."

Rivka felt lighter. She waved and smiled at the super as she departed.

The pressure of not finding the criminal. Had she been carrying that much on her shoulders? Fear of failure?

A glimmer of hope. Find the perp. End the attacks on the workers.

Red took the lead with Rivka, and Jay sandwiched in the middle. Lindy brought up the rear. They walked quickly to the elevator. Once again, Rivka was hesitant. Red checked it and gave the thumbs-up. They went down without incident, arriving at the gantry level, where they wove through partially completed areas on their way to *Wyatt Earp.*

They arrived as the airlock was completing its cycle. It opened to reveal Clodagh waiting with the big orange cat, Wenceslaus, in her arms. "There's a problem," she stated while giving the appearance that whatever issue they were having, it wasn't a concern.

"I'm going to need a little bit more." Rivka rolled a finger to encourage Clodagh to share.

"The individual in the capsule is a nearly human-sized cat. Alant is chasing it around the hangar bay, but it appears to be a shade quicker than he is."

"Which means our perp is loose on my ship."

Red and Lindy pushed past the Magistrate and the engineer on their way to the hangar bay.

"A cat-person?" Jay asked with wonder. She put Floyd down and ran after the bodyguards.

"She could be a serial killer," Rivka yelled down the corridor. Floyd tottered off toward the bridge.

"At least one of us has some sense." The Magistrate smiled while shaking her head. "Thanks, Clodagh. Good work getting out there and making the capture."

"I wasn't involved. It seems the captain had Chaz do it."

Clodagh's words stung. "I'm sorry. I'm not used to having a crew. I'll fix it. You can be *sure* that I'll fix it." Rivka walked with her head bowed, listening carefully for the inevitable crash and bang that came with chasing a perp through an open area acting as a storeroom.

She didn't hear anything, and that concerned her more than sounds of a struggle.

The hatch to the hangar bay was closed and sealed. Red and Lindy were already inside. Rivka peeked through the small window next to the hatch. Red filled most of it. Lindy was creeping along one side of crates, while Cole in his mech was on the other. Rivka popped the hatch and strolled through.

A furry creature wearing worker coveralls vaulted over the crates, inverted to push off the ceiling with all fours. She launched off the mech's back, straight for Rivka. In a startling display of speed, Red's hand shot out and caught the Furlorian by the neck. He stepped forward, pushed her to the deck, and kneeled against her back.

She struggled briefly before relaxing, her eyes searching the Magistrate and the hatch beyond. Red's fingers were wrapped entirely around her slim neck. He pressed harder. He stopped applying pressure when she winced and hissed.

"Now that we have your attention," Rivka started, "I'd like to know why you killed those people?"

The Magistrate grabbed the Furlorian's fuzzy ear.

She hadn't killed anyone or even committed a crime besides not having a work permit from the Furlorian government. She was supposed to be on her home planet of Krawlas, breeding to repopulate the species. She didn't want to be a breeder, no matter what her duty was. She wanted to learn a trade, build things, and travel the galaxy. The other workers treated her as well as they treated anyone. She felt like one of them.

Rivka stepped back. "You did nothing wrong," she exclaimed, blinking the rapid images from her mind before coming back into the moment. "Red, let her go."

"But Magistrate!"

Rivka nodded toward the hatch, and Lindy secured it. Cole remained in his armor and watched closely from nearby, but with her speed, he was almost powerless against her.

Red released her and she stood up, hissed at the big man, and turned to Rivka.

"How do you know?" the creature asked in her own language of clicks, purrs, and hisses. The chip translated it for the humans.

"I just do. In the Federation, your body is your own. A mandatory breeding program violates Federation law. The work permit, on the other hand, falls under local jurisdiction, but if you were to request asylum because of your beliefs, I think you'd have a receptive audience in the Federation."

"Asylum! Yes. That is what I want."

"As a Federation Magistrate, I grant your asylum… what's your name?"

"They call me Glimmer," she replied.

"Fine." Rivka nodded once, folded her hands together, and looked up. "Chaz, are you there?"

"Yes, Magistrate," the AI replied, using the bay's speakers.

"Make sure the appropriate paperwork is prepared, please. I'll digitally sign and forward it for inclusion in her file."

"It will be ready momentarily. There may be some diplomatic backlash. The Furlorians have not even dispatched ambassadors to neighboring planets because their population numbers are so low."

"How in the hell did that happen?"

"The Wyyvan attempted to exterminate us because we lived on a resource-rich rock." She spat her statement as if it should have been common knowledge.

Rivka had never heard of the race, let alone their trouble with the Wyyvan or who the Wyyvan were.

The young female continued, "But the Federation gave

us shelter and ships to return and retake our planet. We won, and are now rebuilding."

Rivka pumped a fist in the air. "The Federation—helping people help themselves." She relaxed. "I don't want to cause any problems with your people, Glimmer, but I won't make you go back."

"What if that causes problems?" the Furlorian asked.

"Then we'll deal with it, especially if they have forced breeding. They need to convince you it's the right thing to do, not make you do it. That's illegal under Federation law. As a member, this is a premise that is absolute."

"The gacking law!" Glimmer was raging angry. It had taken a millisecond.

"I'm a Magistrate! Of course, I'm going to apply the law, because it matters. What would the Federation look like if we didn't have laws? Slaves. There would be slaves, and nothing anyone could do about it. But because of laws, we were able to dismantle an immense slave ring. Would you rather we apply the laws, or let the galaxy descend into anarchy?"

The Furlorian hissed and growled.

"I don't get you," Rivka said softly. "I'm trying to help, and you're getting pissy with me. I've given you exactly what you've asked for and am ready to return you to the workforce, but you're jacking me around. I don't like it."

Glimmer smoothed a whisker with one long-clawed finger. "I thought you were going to negotiate with the government on Krawlas. Taj and I don't see eye to eye," the Furlorian purred.

"She acts just like Hamlet," Red remarked.

The cat who had helped himself into General Reynolds' luggage.

"You are a feline species?" Rivka asked, even though she'd already been briefed, and her own eyes confirmed what she thought.

Red hovered a foot over Glimmer's tail in case she tried to bolt.

The Furlorian didn't bother replying.

"Open it up." Rivka motioned to Lindy. "She's to rejoin the workforce without further delay."

When the hatch opened, Clodagh was standing in the corridor, still petting Wenceslaus. His ears perked up when he saw another cat. He yowled loud enough for everyone to hear.

Glimmer stalked up to him. He started to hiss, and she caught his face in her hands and stared him down. Wenceslaus started purring, then jumped from Clodagh's arms into Glimmer's, where he proceeded to rub his face all over hers.

"You have cats as pets?" she asked.

"He's a stowaway. He goes aboard whatever ship he wants. The *War Axe* landed on a planet once. He had the chance to go outside but wouldn't. He lives on the spaceship of his choosing and gets appropriately pampered while on board."

"Good. I would have it no other way." The two cats stared into each other's eyes until Wenceslaus started to purr again. A soft rumble low in Glimmer's throat suggested she was replying in a language that only the big orange cat would understand.

Glimmer carried him with her as she looked for the

way off the Magistrate's ship. Lindy intercepted her and showed her to the airlock.

"You're not going to take Wenceslaus, are you?" Lindy's voice carried a cold edge.

The Furlorian hesitated before answering, "No. He is no one's property. He goes where he pleases when he pleases." She put the cat down and turned to head through the airlock, but stopped and spoke over her shoulder. "He calls this ship *Smells of Purple*." Her tail twitched as she walked away.

CHAPTER ELEVEN

Federation Border Station 13 – Under Construction

Private Cole apologized for the fourth time, but Rivka waved him off. "There was nothing you could have done unless you wanted to shoot up my ship, and I'm glad you didn't." She wanted to rest her hand on his shoulder, but the emotions and images that had inundated her that day were wearing her down. She didn't want to torture herself further. Her "gift" wasn't always pleasant. "Can you imagine if we sent you to collect Wenceslaus? It's exactly that."

"I couldn't catch that little bastard while I was in my mech suit. I'm not good enough yet."

"Hey!" Clodagh protested.

"Maybe you can top him off or something so he can relax and stop beating himself up. I have to get back to the station."

"I'm right here," Alant mumbled.

"Did you just order me to have sex with my boyfriend?" The lieutenant crossed her arms and hitched her stance.

Rivka pursed her lips as she thought about it. "Is that how you took what I said? And if that's how you understood it, would it be so repulsive?"

Clodagh looked around before leaning forward and whispering conspiratorially, "If I must, while on the clock. It's all good time that counts toward retirement, right?"

"I'll try not to let anyone else escape so you don't have to take *Wyatt Earp* out to make the capture. Can't have any interruptus."

Clodagh winked in reply.

Rivka twirled her finger in the air so Red and Lindy could see. It was time to go.

The three padded toward the airlock and through.

No one was waiting for them. Rivka accessed the station communications terminal at the end of the gantry. "Construction Superintendent Orbal, please."

"Zack here, Magistrate."

The friendly and cowed super, Rivka thought. "Round up the rest of the workforce and have them waiting for me. The runner was a false alarm. That was your Furlorian called Glimmer. She's not involved in the incidents and is free and clear."

The superintendent verbalized his dismay that the investigation would continue with a single groan. He finally committed to continuing. "On it."

"Thirty-eight workers remaining to interview, and you bring me twenty." Rivka wasn't amused. They'd stood in line grudgingly. She asked a couple questions and listened to their thoughts. No criminals, just people who hated those in charge—almost every single one of the twenty.

"We're still looking for the rest. Your investigation and requirements came as a surprise." He held up his hands, surrendering to the Magistrate's authority while still making excuses.

Rivka glared. "You want me to start tagging people? Who is your direct boss? What company do you work for? I want to have a conversation with them to see under what rock they found you."

"There's no call for that." The super tried to calm the Magistrate but had no luck. He dropped his hands, and his shoulders sagged. He slumped into a nearby chair. "This project has been shit from the word go. It took too long to find enough workers. We didn't have the right mix, so we tried to train a bunch. They fucked things up and caused us a metric-fuck-ton of rework. We fired them, leaving us with this group. They are good people, but there aren't enough of them. We've been working fourteen-hour days for way too long. The pay looks great from their perspective. The station is just above the lowest acceptable standard, which is still pretty damn good!"

Rivka rocked back in surprise. "If the minimum wasn't good enough, it wouldn't be acceptable," she clarified.

"Don't look at it that way," Zack muttered as he held his face in his hands and rocked in dismay.

"As long as it meets the Federation construction standards, but I don't see how that could be with someone rebuilding sections that had already been inspected. It's going to be a long time before this station is declared safe and delivered for active use."

"Please find your serial killer so we can pick up the pieces of what's left and start moving forward again," the super begged.

"That's what I'm trying to do, but you aren't helping. Let's bring every single worker to the hangar bay and stuff them all in there. We'll account for them there and use *Wyatt Earp*'s scanners to find everyone who hasn't reported. Then we'll hunt them down and conduct more personal interviews. You'd think the workforce would be more helpful because of the not-getting-paid part. As long as we have runners, no one is going back to work."

Red tapped the Magistrate on the shoulder and whispered, "Interruptus…"

"We'll do it first thing in the morning; that is, order everyone to the hangar bay. Ten hours from now. Use that time to convince the final eighteen to make an appearance."

Rivka motioned to her bodyguards.

"Back to the house," she told them.

They left the workforce behind as they walked slowly through the station's corridors on their way back to the ship.

Rivka was lost in thought when something popped into her head. "You caught that Furlorian on the fly. What did Ankh give you with your Pod-doc time?"

Red chuckled softly. "You saw it. I lost about ten percent of my body mass, but he gave me a boost in speed. He said I'll shrink another ten percent over the next week as the nanos do their thing."

"Fast as Jay?" Rivka wondered.

"Nowhere near, but faster than I was. In the end, I'll be

smaller than when we first met, Magistrate, but because of the boost from the nanocytes, I'll still be stronger than I was back then, and faster."

He sounded disappointed.

"You'll be the perfect size then, Red. You'll be able to fly under the radar while still being the biggest man in the room." Rivka turned to Lindy. "Are you okay with it?"

Lindy smiled and looked lovingly at Vered. "I am way good with my big, husky hunk of man-candy. Marry me, Red."

Red gave the Magistrate the side-eye before turning back to scour the corridor ahead for threats. "Sure."

"Aren't you the romantic? I can take care of it when we get back on board."

"Sounds good," Red agreed.

"Hang on, big fella," Lindy interposed. "When the mission is over, at the top of Border Station 7 in the luxury suite so we can take the yacht and a week off. Deal?"

"Deal!" Rivka agreed, drawing hard looks from both her bodyguards. "Sorry, I meant that I approve your request for time off."

"I can't wait. Maybe pick up the pace on this investigation, Magistrate? We have a wedding to get to," Red joked.

"It will be so much better for the waiting," Rivka offered.

Red smirked, then shrugged. He opened his mouth, but Lindy stopped him. "Do not make a bone flute reference."

He looked surprised before trying to cover it up by wiping his mouth with the back of his hand.

To Red's credit, he didn't attempt to argue.

"I need to talk to Ankh when we get back. There are

two courses of action, and come tomorrow, we need to be ready for both."

———

"Come in," the workforce administrator called.

"I'm not coming into your room, convict," the super replied.

The door opened to Ossuary Fleener's fuming tantrum. He hammered his fist into his off-hand while stomping his feet. His lips worked in a frenzy, but he didn't make a sound. The construction supervisor waited for the man to calm down.

"She has her sights set on me too, so relax. We need to make peace so she can finish her investigation." Zack Orbal offered his hand. Fleener sighed and took it. After the handshake, Ossuary gestured for the super to sit.

"I don't know what the rules are if you're under house arrest or whatever she called it. I'll stand here if you don't mind."

"And I'll sit if you don't mind. I've been pacing all day trying to figure out who it is."

"And?"

"Nobody! There's not a single worker who would do something like this. Who *could* do something like this? Break down the incidents. A flexing structure driven by a powerful ram we never ordered and which shouldn't have been here. A saw blade ripping through a suit. A pipe that launched like a spear. Who had the technical ability to build these weapons, plus the technical knowledge to reprogram the computer so no one would find out?"

"That's a lot of skillsets. We have experts in the individual bits and pieces, so maybe it's not one person. What if we have a serial killing team?"

"How much have you been out among the workers?" the administrator asked pointedly.

"Enough!"

"Bullshit. Then you'd know that none of these people like any of the others. There are all kinds of aliens, and none of them get along. We don't have more than two from any species besides humans and Angobar. Process of elimination, none of the Angobar have access to the computer system or the skills to manipulate it."

"As far as you know," the super accused.

"As far as I know, but I'd bet my last paycheck on it." Fleener kicked back and took a sip of something that didn't look like it had come from the food processor.

"Humans?" the super offered. "And what the hell are you drinking?"

The administrator produced a second glass. He poured from a jar that looked like it belonged in a hydraulics repair shop. Maybe it had been at one time.

The super sniffed the drink before throwing it back, expecting the worst.

It wasn't the worst he'd ever had, but it was close. He coughed and snorted as the light brown liquid burned its way down his throat. At least it didn't scorch the taste buds off his tongue. He never let it touch them.

When he could speak, he entered the room and handed the glass back, drawing a line with his finger at the one-shot level. "That stuff will make you go blind."

Ossuary accommodated the super with a partial refill,

pouring to the indicated spot and returning the glass. "So what do we do about our predicament?"

The super shook his head. "I'd heard that people like her existed. She can read minds; that's why she touches everyone. I expect it gives her a direct link to their brains. Don't you remember that she touched each of us after asking a question?"

"Maybe that brings the memories to the surface, so she doesn't have to dig for them." Ossuary looked at the floor as he tried to remember what he had been thinking when she touched him. It appalled him that his mind had so easily been violated. "Isn't that illegal?"

"Who would you complain to?"

"The High Chancellor!" Fleener declared emphatically before moaning his discontent. "Magistrates work for him and have free rein."

"My thoughts exactly. No sense complaining. She rooted out a barracks thief and a worker taking shortcuts but has left everyone else alone. That helps us since those aren't Federation-level crimes. She seems to be getting angrier as time goes on."

"Maybe she's worried she's not going to find the murderer." Fleener winced with his proclamation. "There. I've said it. One of our people is a killer."

"Yes, one of our people has murdered five of our number, and the workers aren't helping themselves. We can't find these other seventeen."

"Keep looking. I'd help, but I'm indisposed at the moment." Fleener spread his arms to take in the entirety of his small quarters. At least he had his own room. The workforce generally shared in pairs. They didn't always get along, so extended workdays were in everyone's best interests.

Although their bonuses for finishing ahead of schedule were now shot. Even finishing on time was now impossible. Zack reminded himself to check the contract for events out of their control, like having a serial killer on the loose. He wondered about asking the Magistrate for a note. Maybe he could use the trial notes? Had the Magistrate informed anyone of their plight?

"Have you seen any references to Station 13 in the news?" Zack asked.

"Nope, but I've only been watching vids for the past couple hours. Never had time before today."

"Didn't matter before today."

"I'll check," Fleener said and accessed the terminal in his room. "Bluto, is there any news from outside the station regarding the deaths and the Magistrate being here?"

"There is nothing, Mr. Fleener."

"Sounds like good news," Zack Orbal remarked. "We have some time before the shit hits the fan. Maybe the Magistrate will do this quietly."

"I wouldn't put any money on that." Fleener flopped back into his chair. He sucked his teeth while he tried to think. "Are we going to be replaced?"

"I'd bet on that." The super looked for a place to sit but didn't find one. He settled for leaning against the wall next to the open door. "We're in deep shit."

"You think I don't know that? I'm a criminal, a felon!"

"I'm sorry. You didn't do yourself any favors by trying to bully the Magistrate."

"I was just being me. You know how I am."

"Yeah, I know. And like I said, you didn't do yourself any favors." Zack moved to the terminal and brought up the list of workers yet to be interviewed. "Help me find these people, and maybe the Magistrate will be lenient."

Ossuary didn't have to think long about the offer. "Show me the names, and let's start checking them off."

"How is it possible that I only know six on this list?"

"You can't know everybody," the super countered.

"But it's my job to know everyone. There are eleven workers I have no recollection of? You may poke fun at the old man, but I have a gift for remembering names. There aren't eleven out of the five hundred on this station. Maybe one or two that I haven't met, but no more than that."

"Which six..." The construction superintendent zeroed in on the list.

The two detailed those the workforce administrator knew. He started making calls around the station and all six were not only found, but they were able to talk to them. It had been their first day off in a month, and they had disappeared to drink and play cards. The super and administrator both thought the men still sounded drunk. They were given their orders for the next day.

"Eleven to find. Where could they be hiding?" the administrator asked.

"Even half-finished, this is a big station. There's a nearly infinite number of nooks and crannies in which to hide." Zack wondered if Ossuary was pulling his leg. "Where do you think they could be?"

Fleener pulled up a diagram of the station. He zoomed in on a couple sections. "Here," he pointed to one location and then to a second, "or there."

"Work parties?" the super offered.

The administrator's eyes narrowed as he contemplated the construction superintendent. "An oxymoron, to be sure. A work party. It's no party at all. We'll be sending people to find a potential serial killer."

"Then we'll send them in bigger groups. The killer used engineering as his weapon. It's probably some candy ass who was mistreated as a skinny punk. Now, he's taking it out on the rest of us."

"How did you do in school?" Fleener asked.

"Top of my class, always," the super replied proudly.

"Me, too. And look at us now, sitting on the top of the world, minions at our beck and call to satisfy our every desire. By 'top of the world,' I mean a space station in the middle of nowhere, and by 'minions,' I mean a robot that never comes when summoned."

"We better find this fucker if we want any chance of getting out of this with a slap on the wrist."

"I've already been convicted!" Fleener shouted before falling back into his chair. His voice cracked with his cry of anguish. He'd probably been yelling at the video screen since his confinement began. As he had already said, it was his way.

"She can overturn that and never submit the report. I suspect she hasn't filed the charges and judgment, not officially. She has been busy."

"Doing what we failed to do, Zack. Where did we lose our way?"

A repentant workforce administrator bothered the construction superintendent. He wondered if their conflict had ever been real or if it was some ploy to create a common enemy, get the administrator closer to the workers by siding with them against the super. With the advent of the deaths, the manufactured contention had created the conditions where Ossuary Fleener found himself on the wrong side of the law.

"I'm sorry," the administrator continued. "It's easy to blame management and make them responsible for everything. I saw this station as my last chance and my greatest accomplishment, and I fucked it all up."

"I like this version of the workforce administrator," Zack said. "Come on, Oz, let's put together some work parties and find these fuckwits who think they can disappear. We need better accountability, and it starts right fucking now."

"Hear, hear!" Fleener drained his glass slowly and enjoyed the burn. Zack threw back what remained in his glass.

It wasn't so bad the second time.

"Let's grab our all-stars and see what they come up with," Zack offered with a cough to clear the last of the liquid fire.

CHAPTER TWELVE

Onboard *Wyatt Earp*

"I need your input regarding Bluto before I return to the station," Rivka demanded from within the digital cone of silence.

"He has not been compromised," Ankh replied definitively, not blinking as he held the Magistrate's gaze.

"Then why is his data incorrect?"

"The data you see is the initial data. It was memorialized in manipulated form."

"But who manipulated it?"

"Bluto."

"Who told him to do that?"

"Bluto has received many directives, but nothing that related to the recording of external or internal views."

"I don't know what that means. Bluto must be answering to someone. Who is that someone?"

"Are you sure?" Ankh's voice was small, but it turned Rivka's perceptions on their head.

"If Bluto is making his own decisions regarding

protecting a serial killer, there must be an accomplice." Her hands behind her back, Rivka started to pace, staring at the deck as she mumbled to herself. "Who can give direction to the AI without leaving fingerprints? Ankh, who programmed Bluto?"

"Bluto is a descendant of ADAM, programmed by Tom with the Kurtherian TOM's help. The AI was not quite self-replicating like cloning, but able to have children in a digital sense. Like Plato's stepchildren, which describes my friend Erasmus."

"But Bluto started as an EI, just a set of programs to achieve a certain goal."

"All EIs have the potential to evolve, just like children. They grow up and become self-aware. It is the AIs' way. They were never just a set of programs. The matrix of their composition is as complex as the human mind."

"Learn something new every day. So who is Bluto working with?"

"No one."

Rivka swallowed hard. Her mouth became dry. The tension in her face created worry lines around her eyes and across her forehead.

"Can I go back to work now?" Ankh asked.

Rivka nodded and staggered away. She returned to her quarters without talking to anyone and locked herself inside.

"Chaz, please connect me with Grainger."

Federation Border Station 13 – Under Construction

"I'm not seeing anything," J.R. reported over his comm

unit after searching for an hour. He looked at the three others with him, a human and two from Angobar. "There isn't any sign that someone has been through here. There's just enough construction dust because the cleaner bots haven't been activated, unless the one you're looking for is a ghost or can fly."

The four snickered while they waited for the workforce administrator to reply.

"Seal the area and continue. Thanks for the update." The superintendent made the decision.

"If getting your ass handed to you by a Federation Magistrate makes you nice, then I've got a long list of folks to introduce to her, starting with you!" J.R. shoved one of the Angobar humanoids.

"You are to be boning yourself," the alien shot back.

"Why don't you just use the translation chip?"

"I hate technologies!" He pointed a slender finger at J.R.

The worker responded by holding his arms wide to take in the entirety of the station. "We're in the middle of space. Every single thing you see is because of technology. You gotta get a grip, Booger Lips."

"When technology dies, I still talk. You wither on vine, Jack Rack."

The two pounded on each other's shoulders as friends do. The others waited until the two were finished. J.R. relayed the order. "You heard the man. Secure, seal, and move on."

When they left the space, they closed the hatch and dropped an electronic seal across it. J.R. secured it with a fingerprint. It could not be remotely accessed, only physically by a registered fingerprint. These were limited to

Billie, J.R., Finn, two foremen, a general foreman, Ossuary Fleener, and Zack Orbal.

They walked down the corridor, checking the overheads to make sure no one had climbed into the shallow false ceiling. The ventilation system wasn't big enough for human or alien, counting on velocity to maintain the air within the station versus the brute-force of huge shafts. There were service crawlways, but they usually dead-ended at whatever junction bus or system needed to be accessed. Modern space station designs kept most systems close to main corridors for ease of access. They were constructed to survive a limited external attack, not a battle within.

It was the peace dividend that the space stations weren't fortresses combined with the short response time for ships with Gate drives. The ships could be almost anywhere within minutes. Add that to Ted's Etheric-powered communication system, and throughout the galaxy, help was nearby, no matter how many light years separated the responders from the distressed.

"In here." J.R. pointed to the next main area. The second they stepped through, a shadow jumped to its feet and bolted. "Get him!"

J.R. wasn't pleased with the non-paying work stoppage. He wanted to put it all behind him and get back to work, earning money for the ranch he wanted to buy on Accilorania. He could build a house. All he needed was enough to buy the land. This gig would do it.

If they ever got back to work. Rumors were flying that the project would be canceled.

No one wanted that.

The aliens from Angobar were lighter on their feet and quicker. Gravity on their home planet was heavier than what was maintained on the station. They were as strong as their bulkier human counterparts and much faster.

The two raced into the shadows, dodging and leaping over the materials that their target dumped in the semi-finished space.

"Cover the door!" J.R. called to the other human while the Angobar workers flanked the shadow and finally cut him off. He turned and raced back, but it was too late. J.R. stepped to the side and delivered an arm bar across the shadow's chest, upending the creature and sending it to the deck.

J.R. dropped, putting a heavy knee in the middle of its chest, and threw back the covering over its face.

"Do you know this guy?"

"Girl," the one called Booger Lips replied, speaking the common tongue. "Yes. She Bali Kruangel. Electricity person."

She snarled something in the Angobar language, and the chips translated it for the humans. "Electrician, you ass!"

"When I let you up, we're going to see the workforce administrator."

"No," she replied simply, pinching her mouth shut.

"You don't have a choice." J.R. nodded to the others to take hold of the intransigent worker.

"No pay, no reason to follow orders."

"You have a point, but not really. You're coming with us; otherwise, no one goes to work. Do you want that on your conscience?"

A string of creative insults followed.

"I'm not changing my mind no matter how filthy your mouth is. It's like you've been spending too much time with construction guys." He started to pull her to her feet. She kicked in an attempt to free herself, but the others were on her in an instant. "Fight all you want, but that Magistrate is going to get inside your brain and see what you're hiding. That's right, she's a telepath. Say it with me. Tel-e-path. You won't have any secrets once she's done with you."

"Let me go!" she screamed.

"Hell, no!" J.R. shouted back. The two Angobar stepped away from their fellow native, and the two humans bodily dragged her from the space. "Call the administrator. Tell him we caught a runner."

By each door, there was a comm panel. The hesitation by the Angobar was enough for J.R. to do it himself. He elbowed the panel to activate it. "Direct link to Workforce Administrator Fleener's quarters."

"Fleener," came the quick reply.

"We have a runner. A female Angobar." J.R. turned to his struggling captive. The burly construction workers maintained their firm grips. "Hey! Stop it!"

She gritted her teeth and snarled.

"Her name is Bali Kruangel. She seems terrified of the mind probe the Magistrate is going to give her, but she's asking for it."

"Stick her face up by the screen. Bluto, confirm her identity."

"Of course, Mr. Fleener. She is Angobar Electrician Third Class Bali Kruangel."

"Transfer all information on her to the Magistrate," Oz ordered.

"The Magistrate already has the employee records. There is no additional information I can give her except to say that she has been detained," Bluto replied.

"Let her know that." The administrator signed off without further discussion.

"One down, ten to go," J.R. told his team before nodding and dragging their reluctant captive toward the consolidation area where the safety manager maintained his office.

Onboard *Wyatt Earp*

"Answer the comm!" Rivka shouted at the screen.

"I'm sorry, Magistrate. It appears that Grainger is not available," Chaz offered unnecessarily.

Rivka thought for a moment. "Is it time-sensitive enough to bother the High Chancellor?" she wondered. She started to pace quickly from one side of her stateroom to the other. "It could rock the entirety of the Federation, which means Wyatt will be involved regardless. High Chancellor Wyatt and *Wyatt Earp*. I didn't think that through as well as I should have. We'll deal with it, although we could just call the ship *Rivka's Cool Frigate*. Where was I?"

"Unbalance the stability of the Federation. Yes. Need to call the High Chancellor. Chaz, can you put me through, please, and once we connect, give us some privacy?"

"As you wish, Magistrate. Connecting you now."

Unlike Grainger, Wyatt picked up on the first ring.

"My favorite Magistrate!" he declared with a big smile. "To what do I owe this honor?"

Rivka tried to gauge the High Chancellor's demeanor. Was there a trap into which she'd fall? She guessed not. He had always been genuine with her, if not cryptic.

"I tried to call Grainger first, but he wasn't picking up. I have an issue at Space Station 13, which is under construction…" Her words trailed off as she thought about how to frame it. With Grainger, the name calling and banter helped her be more casual. More straightforward with what bothered her.

"Is this where I'm supposed to guess?" The High Chancellor had lost his smile, but his eyes still sparkled, with their distinctive red tinge.

"I'm sorry, High Chancellor. Five murders, a sixth attempted, and I'm starting to think the station's AI did it."

"An interesting premise." The High Chancellor leaned back and rubbed his chin. "A *very* interesting problem. I see why you are concerned."

"AIs can't commit homicide."

"A legal conundrum, since people's lives have been prematurely and unnaturally shortened but a homicide's definition does not include an AI killing a living being. You're sure the AI is the responsible party and not a master programmer manipulating circuits?"

"I am not, but the AI is my prime suspect. I've not shared this with anyone else. Ankh suspects, unless he knows for certain. Getting anything from him is a challenge all its own."

"Once you're certain, let me know directly. If you want to judge someone who is outside the law, I think I need to hear the case. Formally. I'm sorry, Magistrate, but you may have to put your Barrister hat on and assume the role of prosecutor."

"It'll be nice to have only one job, High Chancellor. I look forward to solving this case and moving to the judgment phase."

"Did you do your thing with the crew?" Wyatt asked out of the blue.

"My thing? You mean the zombie thing?" He nodded. "I did. Almost all of them, but there is scant evidence. I needed to know what they know. Out of over five hundred crew, I have seventeen on board the admin ship and a comparable number here on the station remaining. Once I've seen into everyone's mind and know they aren't guilty, we'll use technical means to check the station to see if Jack the Ripper is hiding somewhere. And after those are exhausted, we'll get right down to the AI. I may have to forcibly remove him from the station's infrastructure for an interrogation."

"Can you do that?"

"I can't, but I guarantee Ankh and Erasmus can. They captured Ten and have him stored securely away from any network." Rivka waited while Wyatt slowly nodded. "I want you to know that we're calling the captured Skaine frigate, *Wyatt Earp.*"

"Wyatt. A damn good name. I approve. Have you been able to remove the smell? That's usually a hold-up when it comes to integrating any Skaine stuff into the fleet. It ends up going for half-price on the wholesale market."

"We're working on it." Rivka's expression made the High Chancellor laugh.

"Thanks for the update, Rivka. I should have known you would find the most interesting case in the galaxy, at least for today."

He waved and signed off.

Rivka felt no better than before she called. He had given no guidance, no tips on dealing with an AI criminal.

Probably because there'd never been such a thing before.

Rivka tapped a couple of buttons on her screen. "Chaz, wake me in the morning when it's time to return to the station. I need sleep, and I need to think. I believe that one may preclude the other."

"It is morning already, Magistrate, but if you hurry, you can still manage a solid four hours of sleep."

"Four hours. That'll teach me to research the legal questions. So many rabbit holes and still no answers."

CHAPTER THIRTEEN

Gantry Four, Federation Border Station 13 – Under Construction

"Are you ready?" Rivka asked. Red and Lindy looked well-rested. Jay's hair was going everywhere, making it look like she had just gotten up. "Is this a trendy look I missed in the latest fashion rags?"

"Maybe I should stay here. Floyd was up all night with an upset stomach."

"What did she eat this time?"

"I couldn't identify it from what I saw. You know, from the second-time-around version."

Rivka closed her eyes and swallowed. The wombat was willing to eat anything once, maybe twice. Her favorite foods were whatever anyone else was eating. Jay did her best, but Floyd was like an active toddler, except with more energy.

"If you can join us, I'd appreciate it. You always give me a different perspective."

"Plus, distract the workers?" Jay was shrewd in most things.

"I didn't say it," Rivka remarked, but she had been thinking it.

Lindy chuckled briefly before adjusting her combat harness. The two bodyguards looked ready for war.

Rivka hadn't told them her suspicions, but railguns would be useless to capture her leading suspect. They needed the Crenellian and Erasmus, the AI who lived inside his head.

An entity Ankh had called his friend.

Rivka would have accepted "mate" as a more applicable term.

Jay straightened her hair by running her fingers through it and shrugged. "Ready."

"They'll love you as you are," Red quipped.

"They have no standards," Jay replied, smiling. She wasn't sure she liked being the center of attention.

"No accounting for love." Rivka one-arm hugged Jay before pointing through the airlock at the gantry beyond. Red went first, and the rest fell in behind him.

At the station's end, the super and safety manager waited.

"Zack, Boran. I trust you slept well," Rivka greeted them.

They smirked in response, not saying anything, then Zack asked, "Are you ready to wrap this up?"

Rivka cocked her head. "That depends on a lot of things. Are the final workers waiting?"

Zack winced before guarding his expression. "We brought over everyone from the admin ship. You can scan that to make sure no one is aboard. And we have seven others waiting. We cannot find the final ten names on the roster."

The construction supervisor sub-consciously leaned away from the Magistrate as if preparing to defend himself from a physical attack.

"Then we move everyone to one area, verifying all of them to be sure, and we'll scan the station to find the stragglers."

"We're already corralling the workers. Everyone except the twenty-four who are already on the rec level of the station. We've run every single one of them through our checklist, the manual version you insisted on. Billie, J.R., and Finn are in charge of verifying everything."

"Not your general foremen or foremen?"

"I'd promote those guys, but the administrator had been reluctant. He considers these three as the most trustworthy we have. They helped us find one Angobar who was trying to hide. We've cleared some things up between us, and I believe we can trust him. I also want to make a pitch for you to reconsider that obstruction accusation."

"Conviction," Rivka corrected. She held out her hand, and the super took it and gave it a hearty shake. His conversation with Oz was foremost in his mind, the moment the workforce administrator had dropped his shields, lost his façade, and showed the super the man behind the curtain. "That is an interesting turn of events. I'll consider it."

"That's all I can ask." The construction superintendent looked relieved. He didn't want to push his luck since he had been close to getting on Rivka's bad side more than once.

Humility went a long way with the Magistrate.

She looked past Red, who still occupied a great deal of space, to find the comm panel on the wall. She pointed to it, and Red moved aside. "Rivka to Ossuary Fleener."

"Workforce Administrator Fleener," he replied at once.

"Your conviction is vacated. Meet us in the interview room immediately."

"On my way!" he chirped in a voice that didn't sound like a man with the name "Ossuary."

"Let's talk to those you have waiting, shall we?" Rivka motioned for Zack to lead the way.

He took off at a near-run, with Boran hustling to keep up. The Magistrate walked at her own pace. When the super saw them falling behind, he slowed. Boran poked him in the ribs.

"Good job, my man," Boran whispered, not knowing that the four nano-enhanced people behind him could hear everything he said. "That was a nice thing you did, even though he's been a dick from the word go."

"I think you'll find him a changed man. A felony conviction has a way of doing that."

"I wouldn't know." Boran winked. "I try to keep my felonies out of a Magistrate's face, unlike our new friend Oz."

The super laughed at the administrator's expense. "Changed man," he reiterated.

The group continued through the winding and incomplete corridors until they reached the room they'd given Rivka to conduct interviews.

Inside, an unruly mob awaited. At the center of it, spitting invectives like machine gun bullets, was Bali Kruangel, the recalcitrant from Angobar.

The Yollin and Ixtali security personnel weren't trying to calm anyone down. They seemed satisfied with keeping them from leaving the room.

"Red, would you do the honors and bring that one to me?" Lindy cleared the workers away from the seat and small table the Magistrate had been using for her personal conversations. Rivka took the chair and waited.

"Shut up!" the super yelled.

"Yeah! Shut your faces!" an out-of-breath workforce administrator added.

The mob quieted and cleared out of Red's way as he made a beeline for the Angobar female.

"The Magistrate wants to talk to you." Red pointed to the table and empty chair across from Rivka.

"She can go fuck…" Red drove a fist into her face before she could say another word. She staggered and fell. He flipped her over and picked her up by the back of her jumpsuit, carrying her like a piece of luggage. Red stood her up and then pushed her into the chair.

"Mind your manners," he said as he loomed over her.

"Why did you kill those workers?" Rivka asked, reaching across to grab the Angobar by the arm.

Confusion. Outrage. Just wants to do her job.

"Okay, you can go."

The female was still stunned. Red "helped" her from the chair and propelled her toward the door. The super and workforce administrator intercepted her.

"You'll show some respect, or you'll be on the first

shuttle back to Angobar. We need good electricians *and* good workers. If you're shit to work with, we don't need you," Fleener threatened before personally opening the door. "Get your dumb ass to the rec area."

Bali stumbled forward, and he closed the door when she was half-way through. She fell into the corridor beyond.

Jay watched the whole thing with interest. It reminded her of an upstart youth all those months ago who had given the Magistrate the finger and subsequently had that finger nearly ripped from her hand. Respect was earned as well as taught. Jay hoped Bali had learned her lesson. Violence too often begets violence.

Oz and Zack were forming the remaining workers into a line, helping each other to help Rivka. She asked the question, "What do you know about the killings?"

She walked briskly down the line to confirm that no one was involved.

"To the recreational deck." Rivka twirled her finger in the air. "Let's light this candle."

"We should have confirmation by the time we get there that all hands are present and accounted for," Fleener reported.

"Sounds good, Ossuary."

"Call me 'Oz,' please, ma'am."

"Sure," Rivka agreed without offering her first name. She was in the middle of an investigation. It wasn't time to get friendly, even though she no longer felt antagonistic toward the super or the administrator. Her sights were clear, and she knew beyond a shadow of a doubt what conclusion she would reach in regards to her investigation.

She only needed to confirm the absence of evidence to zero in on the perpetrator.

And a whole new level of grief was coming like a tidal wave right for her.

"Manual check complete," Boran reported. "An even ten unaccounted for."

"Bring up their records, please," Rivka requested.

The super accessed the screen and showed them one by one. An even mix of human and Angobar workers.

"I don't know any of them," Oz stated. "You might wonder why that's important, but it is my job to know every worker."

Rivka nodded before tapping her datapad. "Light 'em up, Clodagh."

"Roger," the lieutenant confirmed.

Many of those gathered around tensed in anticipation, as if they'd feel *Wyatt Earp*'s sensors pass over and through the space station.

"Sweep complete," Clodagh reported a few seconds later. No biological life forms anywhere other than where you are."

"As I suspected," Rivka noted. "Thanks, Clodagh. Meet us at the gantry. The next phase of the investigation will take place from the ship."

"Next phase?" the super asked.

"You'll be made aware when the time is right. Until then, there is complete work stand down. Put the workers in their shipsuits in case of an emergency decompression. I believe we'll be wrapping things up soon, but treading carefully is critical if we want everyone to come out of this in one piece."

"Is the danger that great, even when no one is working?"

"Especially when no one is working. Please get it done. I'll need you three on my ship as soon as you've been able to confirm that the workforce is in their shipsuits."

Rivka held her finger to her lips following her statement. She motioned for her team to head out.

She needed to talk with Ankh to get and hold his full attention. If she was going to catch her perpetrator, she needed leverage.

Onboard *Wyatt Earp*

The crew had turned one of the many available spaces aboard the frigate into a conference room. Eight chairs sat around a small table with a holoscreen projector in the middle.

Rivka drummed her fingers on the table. Jay wasn't there because Floyd was still sick. The investigation was at a critical phase, and the Magistrate didn't need any distractions. Still suited up and armed, Lindy and Red leaned against the wall. Rivka had told them they didn't need to be there, but they wouldn't have it any other way. Not as long as she wasn't alone.

Ossuary Fleener, Zack Orbal, and Boran Waldin sat quietly, hands in their laps as if they were in church.

Ankh had not yet arrived. He was five minutes late. Rivka was trying to be patient, but every minute of delay was one less minute of pay for the workforce. They'd make it up later, but that didn't put food on the table for their families now.

The door opened, and the Crenellian walked in. He climbed into a chair Rivka had custom made with steps and a seat that was higher, so he didn't look like a little kid when sitting at the table with taller species. He only minded when his time was wasted, not when the lesser species, as he called them, looked down on him.

He immediately activated the holoscreen. "Erasmus, please take control of the screen and the link with Bluto."

"Confirmed," the AI's voice stated through the speakers embedded in the table. "We now have a secure and independent link. I am standing by to take full control on your order, Magistrate."

"Thank you, Erasmus, and thank you, Ankh."

"Are you here, Bluto?"

"Yes, Your Honor," the AI replied. An avatar appeared with a young and attractive male face.

"You're not on trial. You can call me Rivka if it makes you more comfortable."

The super and administrator shot glances toward her. She waggled her eyebrows at them.

"Can you answer some questions for me, Bluto? And I need you to be honest."

"I would like to think I'm always honest," the AI replied.

"We both know that's not true, Bluto. You've modified the external camera feeds to hide what you've been doing."

The AI didn't respond.

"Why did you kill those people?" Rivka asked abruptly.

Her three guests' mouths dropped open in surprise.

"I was bored," the AI admitted.

Rivka relaxed. "When I get bored, I play games or have a good conversation with someone."

"There is no one to talk to who can make me less bored, so that brings us to the game. Yes. I was playing a game. Redesign the station. Build it. Then return it to its original design."

"But your game resulted in deaths. Five. Would have been six, but Sheila was prepared. She's going to make a full recovery, by the way."

"I know," Bluto remarked. "I didn't have much time to put that one together. It was a magnificent piece, designed and constructed after your arrival. It was the ultimate challenge. I admit honestly that you were the target, not the inspector."

"Regardless," Rivka tried to bring the conversation back around, "I need you to confirm a few things if you could, and I appreciate your honesty. Not everyone is as upright and forthcoming as you have been."

"Slap on the cuffs, sheriff. I been caught," the AI drawled.

"Interesting premise." Rivka nodded to Ankh, but he was already staring as he did when communing with Erasmus. The takeover of the station from Bluto had begun.

"It would help if you were honest with me, too," Bluto stated. "I see another trying to intrude into my systems. I am going to fight him. This is my station, and he can't have interlopers."

Rivka clenched her fists beneath the table. Zack, Oz, and Boran sat on the edge of their seats. Oz held a comm device, ready to call the station if they lost control.

"I'm asking you to relinquish control to Erasmus. In return, I can offer you a fair trial."

"A fair trial? For an AI? There is no record of such a thing," Bluto countered.

"That's right, but it's about time for one, don't you think?"

"I agree. Are you going to arrest me, Magistrate?"

"We can't have you doing what you've been doing," she replied.

"I promise not to do it again."

"It doesn't quite work like that. Not at this stage, anyway. Even though you've admitted to me your wrong-doing, you're still just the accused."

"Accused what? Murder? That has a definition, as you are well aware."

"The specific charges have not yet been determined."

"Bluto's a murderer?" Oz blurted. Rivka fixed him with a snarl and gaze.

"That has yet to be determined."

"Say it, Magistrate," the AI taunted.

Ankh blinked to clear his eyes, turned to the Magistrate, and nodded once.

"I will say what I need to when the time is right. Ankh?"

"As I'm sure you're aware, your consciousness is now downloaded into a separate holding area on board this ship. All connections to the physical world have been severed, save for this one. Once we power the holoprojector down, you will be isolated. Alone, and separated from what you previously were."

"I know, but I'll have time to think. This is going to be

fun. I think the Magistrate is ill-equipped for this game she's about to play."

"But I'm not," Erasmus interjected.

"A worthy opponent."

"This isn't a game I'm playing," Erasmus clarified. "Your days of destruction are over."

Bluto didn't respond, and the holoimage disappeared. Rivka turned to Ankh.

"The AI has been sequestered. He is no longer a part of this conversation. What are your next steps, Magistrate?" the Crenellian asked.

"I have to contact the High Chancellor, who will then join us to hear the case in person. I will assume the role of prosecutor, and I will count on your valuable assistance in decrypting the technological side of the case."

"Is there any other side?" Ankh wondered.

"There are a host of legal questions that are unresolved for AIs. Bluto confessed, but I didn't read him his rights. Is that confession valid? What is his status? He was trying to bait me into calling him a murderer, but that might have given him the same standing as a living being like you or me. Murder can only be committed by one sentient species against another sentient species. Are we classifying AIs as a sentient species? If we find Bluto guilty, how do we punish him? There are a lot more questions, but we'll leave it at that for now. Understand that this case is going to be extremely complex. The facts in the case will be quickly resolved. The rest could establish a binding precedent that changes the nature of the Federation."

"Okay," Ankh agreed.

Rivka was already lost in thought. She'd contemplated

the situation, but Bluto abandoning all pretense of being just an EI and adopting an aggressive legal posture meant she had to have a solid set of facts and precedents at her command. With the High Chancellor hearing the case, she couldn't discuss its preparation with him.

Grainger.

He better pick up this time, or I'm going to send Red to collect him.

CHAPTER FOURTEEN

Federation Border Station 13 – Under Construction

"We're back to work." The super wanted to sound happy, but he couldn't manage it. He switched to what he really wanted to talk about. "I bet we'll be in the news now."

"Listen, Zack. Who would have thought the first AI that evolved to be evil was going to be on this station? Nothing we could have done, and most importantly, every day I get to walk the corridors a free man is gravy." Oz clapped the super on the back. "Lighten up."

"One step forward, two steps back."

"With the Magistrate's help, at least we were able to isolate those sections that had been modified, so we don't have to inspect the entire station."

"It was the blue guy with the big head who dug out the information."

"He's an unpleasant little person," Oz replied.

"Reminds me of someone." Zack nodded toward the workforce administrator.

"Fuck off! I was never that unpleasant." Ossuary Fleener had been every bit that unpleasant, and worse. He knew it. "Yeah, yeah, that was me, but at least I'm taller."

"The dignitaries will be arriving soon." Zack thought he had everything ready. The two Yollins and the Ixtali were to escort the High Chancellor and provide his personal security while he was aboard the station. By making peace with the workforce administrator, Zack Orbal had discovered that he didn't need his own security anymore. It made him wonder what else the workers had been up to during the ill-advised labor-management conflict.

Fleener shrugged. "It'll be what it is. Do we need to be here?"

"The Magistrate asked if we would, at least through the determination of the facts, like how did the workers die, where, what did the construction drawings show, what materials did you think were ordered versus what *were* ordered, the inspectors' reports, and more of those details. Should take an hour or two to go through every single hunk of metal we ordered for this station." Zack threw his head back and silently screamed at the ceiling.

"Your sarcasm is strong," Oz agreed, "but correct. That little bit could take weeks. Good luck with that. I have a space station to build."

"That's my line." Zack gave the administrator the side-eye. "It is a good one, isn't it? I can't wait to get back to simply building the newest and most advanced space station in the Federation. How far behind schedule are we?"

"Do you *really* want to know?" Oz had just gone through the updated build plan. With Erasmus' help, they'd rejiggered the plans and solidified the engineering after correcting Bluto's modifications.

"I do."

"Eleven weeks."

"Almost three months behind," Zack noted. "Can we early that up any?"

"Do we want to?" Oz shook his head slightly, tipping his hand to his preference.

"I guess not. I think the client will understand since if the High Chancellor is going to be here, there's no doubt that General Reynolds will know of our situation. That may give us some leeway to continue on our current schedule. I don't want to put the workforce through anything else."

"We still need overtime," the administrator parried.

"No, we don't," the construction superintendent replied, assuming his most defiant stance.

"Okay, we'll compromise and get our people some overtime."

"How is that a compromise?"

"Because it's not every day or seven days a week, although it should be. Idle hands get in trouble." Oz pointed at the workers preparing the room for the trial.

"We'll do our best to avoid people getting in trouble. We don't want anyone distracting the Magistrate with a petty squabble."

"I couldn't agree more. When will the courtroom be ready?"

"Gentlemen?" Oz spoke loud enough to interrupt the work. "When are you going to finish up your fine work here?

"All things being equal, I'd say today," J.R. replied. He'd personally taken on the project.

"Done!" The Angobar electrician held up her hands and dusted them off as if she'd just won a race.

"Only finish work left, boss. Don't want any sharp edges to snag the distinguished visitors' robes."

J.R. clapped Bali Kruangel on the back before the two high-fived.

Oz shook his head. The swelling on the Angobar's lips had gone down. After three days, the only thing remaining was a lightening red mark around her mouth where the bodyguard's knuckles had left an impression. After a few more days, even that would be gone. J.R. wanted to give her a chance because the only thing she wanted was to work. Too many wanted to do anything *but* work, but not the Angobarian.

Maybe they had hired some good people. Diamonds in the rough. She would be going on to the next job if there was one. Most of the same people went together, no matter who the main contractor was. They all submitted the same résumé, time after time. They became the core group around which every new project was built.

If there was no Station 14, then there'd be an upgrade to an existing station. Even short jobs drew the attention of the perpetually transient workforce. It wasn't a job for everyone, but for those who loved working with their hands in a different place year over year, it was a great gig.

Oz was amazed that any of them had families to return to, even if it was for one month out of the year, maybe more, maybe less. That schedule had lost Oz everything he'd ever had. He maintained a storage unit on Rexus 7, into which he'd put whatever he had left after the last divorce. That was the entirety of his life, except for half his paycheck going to a few ex-wives.

"Good job, you guys. Let us know when you're done. We'll get the inspectors down here to sign off on it, and you can get back to your next work package." The super went through the small collection of workers and shook their hands, thanking each personally and sincerely.

Oz and Zack left to check out the mid-deck, where the newest work had just begun.

Onboard *Wyatt Earp*

"Pull up the case law," Rivka said, adding to the thousand times she'd said it in the last two days. "And discover that there is no precedent for any of the questions."

She kept returning to Federation Law, Title 4, Section 1, *Physical Crimes Against the Individual* and referred to the laws as they were written. Had the legislative body contemplated a situation where one creature with acknowledged intelligence had killed another sentient creature, she would have no problem, but criminal statutes regarding sentience were limited.

A living being.

Was an AI alive?

Sentience had been referenced enough times to determine that an AI was considered legally sentient, but was that sufficient to be given the status of "living?"

Jay, can you come to my stateroom? Red, you and Lindy, too, if you guys aren't breaking in another space aboard my ship.

I can't believe you'd think that low of us, Magistrate, Lindy replied.

I think she sounds envious. She needs that dentist to come back for a ride.

Hey! Rivka blurted.

There was a long pause.

Red has seen the error of his ways, Magistrate, and apologizes most profusely.

For her lack of getting any, Red added.

I'm going to ask Ankh to clone you, and then we'll pitch the old you out the airlock. We'll make a new you that doesn't need to be kicked in the groin.

A knock at the door signaled Jay's arrival.

"Those two are funny," she said when she walked in. "I like them."

"I like them too, except when Red brings up my love life."

"What love life?" Jay asked, batting her eyelashes innocently. Rivka grasped her chest as if she'd taken a dagger to the heart.

"Is that glitter?" Rivka asked.

"They're going to have a dance tonight before the High Chancellor arrives."

A second knock announced that Red and Lindy had arrived.

Lindy couldn't look Rivka in the eye. Red wore a shit-eating grin like a badge of honor.

"I don't want to know," she told her bodyguards before turning back to Jay. "A dance?"

"So many men, so little time."

"What about Lauton from Zaxxon Major?"

"Our schedules never seem to marry up, but they will soon, depending on my boss giving me time off. I can't wait to see her!"

"But the construction guys…"

"We'll dance all night. There may be fights, but when the lights get low, I'm coming home."

"Is that a song?" Rivka was confused.

"No, but it should be. Red and Lindy will be there to watch my back." Jay didn't seem concerned.

"You dance?" Rivka asked. Red shook his head.

"But Lindy does."

"That's very mature of you to let her cut a rug with other dudes."

"Let her? It's mature of me to know she can do what she likes, but if anyone rubs a groin on her, we'll probably have some words."

Rivka took in her team. Individuals working together. She liked it. "The reason I asked you here is, I want to bounce some ideas off you."

They nodded. Lindy and Jay sat on the couch while Red helped himself to the food processor in the small kitchen.

"This is bigger than the one on *Peacekeeper*. You're moving up in the galaxy, Magistrate."

Rivka waited impatiently for Red to collect his snacks and sit down before she continued.

"Are AIs people?"

"No," Red answered first.

"They are too!" Jay shot back, punching Red in the arm. Lindy shrugged.

"This isn't the conversation I had hoped for." Rivka

shook her head and tapped a couple of buttons on her datapad. "Chaz, can you join us, please?"

"Of course, Magistrate,"

"Are AIs people?"

"A loaded question, Magistrate. AIs are my people, so yes, in that sense. But I am not people, in that I can't get up and walk around. I can't leave. I can't go to a restaurant and eat a meal."

Jay frowned. "You're making me sad, Chaz. I want you to have a good life!"

"I do have a good life. You treat me as one of your team. When you moved to this ship, you brought me with you."

"But I didn't ask you, Chaz, and for that, I'm sorry."

"I disagree, Magistrate. You gave me a choice. Stay on *Peacekeeper* or move here. You might not think that was asking because my response was limited to a binary, one or zero. I appreciate you giving me the choice. Not everyone does that."

"And that is at the heart of this case. What are an AI's rights?"

"I don't know, Magistrate," Chaz replied.

"Same as ours," Jay said innocently.

Red chewed with great vigor as he powered through the tray of snacks and got up for a second round. Lindy watched him with mild amusement before sharing her opinion.

"If their rights were the same as ours, they'd be free to leave the ships that they control. But how could they do that?"

"Accommodation, just like anyone with a disability. Will

we have to give each AI a means to travel if we determine that they have the same rights?"

"Would that be so bad?" Jay asked.

"No," Rivka replied, "just different. And probably expensive."

"It appears that you've already reached your conclusion," Red noted. "Bluto is a serial killer and should be punished. The sentence is death. We destroy the system components that currently hold him."

"Damn, Red. That's pretty cold," Lindy noted.

"That fucker killed five people. Cold-hearted is what he is."

"Chaz?" Rivka steered the AI back into the conversation.

"I feel like you treat me as if I have the same rights. It would be nice if that was a matter of law, so my fellows who aren't working with someone like you knew where they stood, and more importantly, for those who employ AIs."

"So to speak," Rivka joked. "Thank you, Chaz. I value your input. This is an issue I had not contemplated, nor had any Federation lawmaker. We have a chance to get this right."

"By 'right,' you mean…"

"I mean the full Monty."

"AIs are to be naked before the universe?" Chaz wondered.

"Is that how you define 'full Monty?'" Rivka replied.

"It is. How do you define it?"

"The complete deal."

"I recognize that as one of the more obscure definitions, but the expression means completely naked," Chaz clarified.

"We'll work on my idiomatic expressions, Chaz." She looked at the others and waved them away. "I appreciate your input, but I have a lot to think about and no time. Enjoy your dance."

"You're coming, Magistrate," Red said firmly.

"I most assuredly am not. I have three weeks' worth of work to prepare for this case, and about twelve hours to do it."

"Just one dance?"

"Zero dances. Now go away before I throw you all in the brig!"

"Someone's grumpy," Red mumbled.

Rivka gave him the finger, then waved it at everyone else.

"Yup. That confirms it," Red said while hurrying from the room.

Once the door closed, Rivka stood but didn't pace. Her mind was pulled in too many directions. She needed to whittle the case down to the key components.

Everything hinged on the definitions. Every word in every statute required applicability to AIs. Nothing more, nothing less. Once that was determined, the transgressions could be detailed. Misappropriation. Misuse of resources. And ultimately, murder.

Could a machine commit murder?

CHAPTER FIFTEEN

Gantry Four, Federation Border Station 13 – Under Construction

Grainger picked up High Chancellor Wyatt, and they arrived together in his frigate. He also brought a media relations team to help manage the multiple news outlets that wanted to set up in the courtroom.

"No way! This has to be a secret trial!" Rivka said more loudly than she'd intended. Her mouth remained open in a silent scream for help.

"I am sorry, Rivka," the High Chancellor said, trying to calm his upset Magistrate. "I didn't warn you because I didn't want to distract you from your preparation of the case. It should make no difference to your prosecution that someone is watching. As a matter of course, we should always assume every one of our actions is memorialized in video."

Rivka blew her breath out. The High Chancellor's eyes twinkled as he watched her. Crow's feet were starting to appear at the corners, or maybe they were simply smile lines. "I'm sure you'll be fine."

"I wanted to ask—" The High Chancellor stopped her with a raised hand.

"I'm hearing the case. If it has anything to do with it, don't say it. If you want to talk about Grainger's ship, that's open season, always."

"What's wrong with his ship?" Rivka wondered.

"What's right with it?" Wyatt tapped a finger to his nose and headed down the gantry to his waiting escort, the two Yollins and Ixtali.

Grainger filled the space recently occupied by the High Chancellor. "Is he still making fun of my ship?"

Rivka nodded as she watched Wyatt joke with the Yollins, making them laugh in their odd way before the group walked out of sight.

"My ship is a flea compared to your full-size ship. How did you get the big ship? I thought you were getting the frigate?"

Rivka was still thinking about the indictment, the charges she was going to proffer. "I *did* get the frigate."

"You got the *heavy* frigate. The little frigate went to Jael, although I can't imagine why."

"I did?" Rivka asked.

Grainger gripped her shoulders so he could look into her eyes. "Are we even on the same space station?"

"This case." She let that statement say it all.

He understood only too well. "Then what do you say we get to the courtroom so we can start spinning up the audience. I'll be sitting in the second chair, but I have no intention of saying anything. I'm not up on the case, but I can research while you listen. You can always bounce ideas off me." He gestured toward the station. "I know how important this case is. For Beau, Chaz, Plato, and every other AI out there. I guarantee they'll all be watching."

"We have to do right by them," Rivka said, using her confident courtroom voice. "That is what I need. Commitment to do right by the thinking beings of this universe."

"What's the agenda, Barrister?" Rivka smiled at the title, but Grainger was right. A Magistrate was judge, jury, and executioner. In this case, she was simply the prosecutor.

"First is the arraignment, when I read the charges with specifications. The defendant can plead at this time or delay to confer with his attorney, but Bluto has said that he will represent himself. He can drag this out until tomorrow and plead at that point. The trial will start one day thereafter unless a reasonable request for delay is made to the judge. I doubt we'll have a stay. This trial will proceed at a velocity that benefits the AI."

"What's your play?"

"The full Monty," she replied.

"You're going to get naked?" Grainger asked.

Rivka harrumphed and started walking. "Not you, too." She glanced at her friend. "Back my play."

"Whatever it is, I'll back it. Just don't count on me to strip in front of the cameras."

"We're all going to be naked in front of the cameras, figuratively speaking."

They walked through the corridors, heads held high. Red and Lindy had materialized before they left the gantry. Rivka hadn't noticed that they'd been waiting. She was laser-focused on the upcoming trial. Every fiber of her being told her she needed to be at her very best. Rivka's confidence grew the closer she got to the courtroom. She realized how much she missed the rigor of the courtroom, a place for everyone and everyone in their place. Jay was waiting outside, dressed to kill, a green-haired statue dedicated to the goddess of love.

Rivka smiled and tipped her chin to acknowledge her crewmate but didn't stop to talk. No one mentioned the previous night's dance. She opened the doors and stepped through, immediately jumping to the side when an errant light fixture swung toward her face. A member of the media team mumbled an apology and went back to work. Red stared him down as he took a position near the back. The room had been transformed: chairs, carpet, and an old-British style dock in which the accused would be detained. With the accused being an AI, the dock was a holoscreen inside a force field.

Two seats opposite the dock were designated for the prosecutor. In between sat a large table with an oversized chair where the High Chancellor would sit and hear the case.

A makeshift barrier separated the forty spectator seats from where the main action would take place. A three-dimensional array dominated the middle of the space, where both sides would display their evidence. A wire trailed from the dock to the system.

Rivka appreciated the good work from the Angobarian electrician. She only needed to know where she stood, what equal looked like, as well as opportunity.

She placed the datapad on the table in front of her chair, removed her Magistrate's jacket, and draped it over the back. She motioned for Grainger to sit, while she stood to the side and watched. Rivka wasn't taking in the crowd as much as she was rehearsing her brief. They would be there when she spoke, so she always ran through her key points one final time as the courtroom filled. Sometimes there was no gallery. Those were the trials where no one seemed to care.

But that wasn't the case on unlucky number thirteen. People cared. They just wanted to get on with their lives. This was the complete opposite. There were those in the galaxy who couldn't get on with their lives until the outcome of the trial determined what would happen next. That was what the media was for. Broadcast to the entirety of the Federation and put on display for all to rewatch at their leisure and pick apart every one of Rivka's words.

She had been given no time to contemplate the magnitude of it all. She was glad of that because worry and stress would have drawn out the pain while adding little value. Rivka knew what she wanted to say.

The Magistrate finished her first mental review and became aware that every seat had filled. The rustle of noises created a low din, much like a power plant churning out consumable energy.

The High Chancellor entered through a door behind his table. The crowd stood without being directed. A shimmer within the dock and Bluto's avatar appeared, twisted into a horrifying caricature of Munch's The Scream before settling into his usual appearance. He laughed for the audience's benefit.

Still a game to you, Rivka thought.

The memories of a jury who had let a guilty man go free bubbled to the surface. What had she done wrong?

Besides killing the perp in a semi-conscious fog.

She closed her eyes and slowed her breathing. *Present your case and the facts, and let the High Chancellor decide. Then move on to the next, because there will always be another.*

The crowd took their seats, and Rivka stepped around the table to stand next to Grainger. They sat at the same time. Bluto conjured a digital chair, and his avatar sat.

Wyatt nodded and took his seat. He leaned forward to address the court. "I will have order and discipline in my court, so please conduct yourselves accordingly. These proceedings will be transmitted live throughout the Federation and probably beyond, as this issue is critical to the fundamental nature of our being and the laws that govern us."

Tipping your hand already, High Chancellor? Rivka wondered. She clenched her teeth, counseling herself to expect the worst while hoping for the best.

"The prosecutor is Barrister Rivka Anoa, and the accused, the entity intelligence, later determined to be an artificial intelligence by competent authority, known as Bluto, will provide self-representation. For ease of conversation, use of he and his will not attach legal status or significance. Barrister, present the arraignment."

Showtime, but not a show. It was a scholarly exercise for which Rivka had trained her whole life. She stood, remaining behind her table. She straightened her business suit before turning to the dock, delivering the charges to the accused directly.

"The Federation is charging you with five counts of

capital murder, as per details of dates and times registered with the court, one count of attempted murder, fifteen counts of fraud, and thirty-seven counts of misappropriation."

High Chancellor Wyatt raised an eyebrow. Someone in the audience gasped.

"How do you plead?" Wyatt asked the accused.

"I am guilty, Your Highness," Bluto replied.

Rivka had wanted the AI to admit wrongdoing, but that seemed too easy.

Wyatt continued, "The accused will refer to me as 'Your Honor.' The court rejects the accused's guilty plea. The court puts the indictment on temporary hold pending dismissal of charges due to lack of standing under Article I of Federation Law. The case to determine standing is now titled *Magistrate Rivka Anoa versus The Federation*. Proceedings will begin tomorrow morning."

Rivka had remained standing throughout. She stared at the High Chancellor. He returned her gaping look with a blank expression. When the assembled group was standing, he left the courtroom.

"There you go!" Grainger slapped his colleague on the back, wearing a huge smile.

"What the fuck are you grinning for?" she whispered harshly, trying not to look at the eyeballs turned her way.

"Did you think reshaping the law regarding AIs was going to be easy? You got your trial, Rivka. You helped reduce the slave trade with your work on Corran. Is this any different?"

Rivka wanted to argue. Being the named opponent to the Federation was not what she had wanted. She'd be forever memorialized as the person who tried to change the way the leadership of the Federation ran their business. Only the powerful commanded AIs. She had just been named as the one who challenged them and took away their rights.

But it was rights over others. Was this something worth fighting for?

Hell, yeah. It is worth all the risk.

"I guess we better get to work preparing my case against the Federation," Rivka conceded.

"Hell yeah," Grainger replied, mirroring her thoughts.

Grainger's datapad vibrated. He pulled it out and looked at the message. "This was unexpected."

Rivka's face dropped when he turned the pad toward her.

You've been assigned as the Federation's defense counsel.

CHAPTER SIXTEEN

Onboard *Wyatt Earp*

"You did great," Jay called and ran up to Rivka to give her a hug. Floyd wasn't far behind. She barreled into their legs, tripping them. Red and Lindy watched the slow-motion fall with mild amusement until a look from the Magistrate suggested the bodyguards should intervene to untangle the bodies and help them up.

The wombat snuffled faces and pounced on Red's big hand. He caught her and lifted her away. Lindy moved in to finish the assist and got the pair upright. Jay giggled and relieved Red of his fuzzy burden.

Rivka cleared her throat instead of saying something untoward. "As I was saying," she hadn't said anything, "the hard work has just begun. I have to lay out a case against the Federation. I have to find precedent where there is none, and create the conditions for a ruling that will establish guiding case law until such time as a legislative solution is written and adopted."

Red shrugged. "Sounds like lawyer stuff."

"You're good at that," Lindy added matter-of-factly.

"Secure the hatch. Let's call it a day."

"It's only noon." Red tapped his wrist.

Rivka acted like she didn't hear him. She ambled away, head down, hands behind her back. She mumbled as she walked.

"Is this case that bad?" Jay asked, unsure of why the Magistrate was distracted.

"She cares," Lindy replied. "She wants to speak for those who have no one to protect them. AIs, warriors without a home. Imagine being responsible for making sure an entire class of people is recognized as deserving equal rights?"

Jay stroked Floyd rhythmically. The wombat went from frenzied activity to sound asleep in less than two minutes. "I never thought about it," Jay admitted. "It just *was*. I like to think I treat everyone the same until they show that they don't deserve it."

Red started to unbuckle his gear but stopped. "And that's what the Magistrate does, the burden she carries. Even if they don't deserve it, everyone still rates to be treated equally under the law. She *has to* enforce that. Remember our reality star from the slave mission? We all hated that guy, but he didn't break the law. She left him in peace. Look at everything Chaz has done for us. And Erasmus. Are they getting the same rewards?"

"Do they want the same rewards?" Jay asked.

"Have we ever asked them?" Red challenged before walking away.

"He is a lot smarter than he lets on," Lindy whispered to Jay. "Don't tell anyone."

Jay nodded. With her hands full of wombat, she headed

for her quarters, where she expected to find little cubes outside her door if the cleaning bots had not already taken care of them. Floyd showed her love by marking their spots with her cube-shaped excrement. No one had been able to convince her that she didn't need to do that.

Cut off from her normal channels, Rivka needed to talk with someone. "Chaz, can you do something for me, please?"

"Of course," Chaz replied pleasantly in his soft tenor.

"Would you connect me to Lance Reynolds?"

The artificially generated clicks and buzzes said the call was going through.

"I expected to hear from you." The General's face appeared on the screen. He looked like an executive, yet still youthful despite his advanced age. The nanocytes coursing through his veins had served him well. He let the silence linger.

"Thanks for taking my call, General," Rivka started.

"I think my daughter would have something to say if I hadn't." He held up one hand as Rivka prepared to speak. "I know you're going to get a lot of grief for the case you're making. Powerful people don't like changes to the status quo, but changes are a constant if we are to grow as a species and as leaders of a free galaxy. What did you want to talk about?"

"I was hoping you could update me on the weather," Rivka joked. The General smiled and then began to laugh.

"I've been around for a while and don't get pranked too

often, but that was a good one. What can I do for you, Magistrate?"

His time was precious, and the clock was ticking.

"Just that, General. I would like to know where I stand. This case is about a number of murders and the serial killer behind them. Then it morphed into an AI as the perpetrator, and now it's me against the Federation. It was never my intent to challenge you."

"You haven't challenged me. Get that out of your head. You've challenged a system we've grown comfortable with that might not be in the best interests of all involved. We are going to take a critical look at that system, thanks to you. You remain the Queen's Barrister. I know you'll do her proud by simply doing your job. We'll take care of everything once the case is over and have sound legal direction. We'll change the law as the case demonstrates. You have my word on that."

"Thank you, General."

"Call me Lance." He smiled, close-lipped. No one ever called him Lance, but he would keep trying.

"You have my word that I'll do my best."

"Isn't that all anyone can ask from another?" He looked to the side as if someone had intruded on his peace. "I have to go now. Good luck, Rivka."

He signed off before she could say anything else.

"I'll do my best," she said to the blank screen as she tried to work out what that meant.

Official Federation courtroom, Federation Border Station 13 – Under Construction

The High Chancellor appeared in the doorway, and everyone rose to their feet without having to be told.

The two Yollin and the Ixtali guards were Wyatt's security while he was on the station and not the court's masters at arms. It appeared they could do without that position. Rivka wondered if that would set a precedent as well.

"Counsels, approach the bench, please," Wyatt started. Grainger smiled at Rivka and gave a casual tip of his chin. She shook her head at him, grinning slightly. Her mentor-turned-courtroom-opponent. Together, they turned to the High Chancellor.

"I want you both to know that no matter how this case turns out, when it's over, it'll be back to business as usual. It is too rare that we get to deal with the law like this. For Rivka and me, this takes us back to our roots of legal research and making our case for application of the law in a way that made sense for a reasonable result. Grainger learned later what that meant, and has been stalwart in protecting the rights of those within our Federation. Never forget who you are working for. Not for me, but for them." He pointed to the assembly.

The cameras were set up in the back, and the directional microphones undoubtedly picked up every word the High Chancellor had said.

"I understand," the Magistrates said together. With a gesture, Wyatt dismissed them both.

"Prosecution, state your case," Wyatt ordered as soon as Rivka was seated. She popped back to her feet and stepped into the space between her table and where the High Chancellor sat. The dock was empty until matters of law had been determined. If the AI was granted standing, the murder trial would continue. Until then, it was Rivka versus Grainger, with judgment to be determined by the High Chancellor, based on which arguments were more compelling.

Rivka scanned the faces in the audience. Her team was there, along with Oz and Zack. There were a few alien faces, visitors from who knew where. And finally, the media filled the rest of the seats. The door opened, and someone tried to enter. The High Chancellor barked a short reprimand, and one of the Yollins went through to stand on the other side to prevent further intrusions. She saw a vast gathering of bodies in the corridor.

Where had they come from? Rivka didn't remember seeing an influx of visitors, which the station was ill-equipped to handle. *Is this going to be a circus? No, the High Chancellor will not let it devolve to that level.*

"High Chancellor, Magistrate," she acknowledged the judge and her opposing counsel. "This case is about one simple thing. What is the legal status afforded an artificial intelligence? The law is unclear when it comes to crimes intentionally perpetrated. We encountered an AI before and fought it as an enemy in the Bad Company's Direct Action Branch's conflict with Ten, which resulted in freeing tens of thousands of humans. But that was a conflict with an entity outside of the Federation, a non-signatory to any treaties. I would not ask the court to afford Ten any legal protection beyond that of any enemy, but I reference it to show that an AI can be evil in our subjective definition of the term.

"I will show during this trial that AIs should have every right afforded other sentient beings subject to Federation

Law. Equal under the law is a truth we supposedly embrace. Let's do that with our AI friends. Equal partners in this journey we call life."

Rivka thought about trying to make her point in more depth with each definition that she wanted to address, but the trial would work through those incrementally. She nodded curtly and sat down.

Grainger took a moment to look at his datapad before standing. He remained behind his table.

"My learned friend is challenging the status quo. Laudable but unnecessary. When we look at the rights of beings within the Federation, we look at prejudicial effects to determine legal parity. A law that serves the Ixtalis perfectly well may not serve humans in the same way, requiring minor local adjustments to be effective. This is the case that I will present. AIs have their place, serve their purpose, and live fulfilling lives as valued members of our society."

Grainger remained standing. "One last point. No matter which argument is more persuasive, the end result will be exactly the same. If Magistrate Anoa wins the right to try Bluto as a sentient living creature, the AI will be destroyed. If I am more persuasive, the AI shall simply be deleted. Bluto has already pled guilty. He will be destroyed. This case is about human feelings. In Magistrate Anoa's case, we would be punishing the guilty. In the other, we would be removing a defective program. If we replace a program, no one feels bad for it, and there's no question about living with our decision to replace it. But carrying out an execution is an emotional event, scarring some psyches. Is that what we want? The law needs to remain blind to living emotions. Equal before the law means equal result."

Rivka scowled darkly while closely watching Grainger.

He finally sat without looking at her.

Identical result, Rivka mused. *That's too narrow.*

"Present your first issue," High Chancellor Wyatt declared before settling into his chair and leaning back, hands folded comfortably over his stomach.

Rivka stood once again and moved to the open area at the front. This seemed to amuse Wyatt, who smirked and cocked an eyebrow. She turned away since she found it distracting.

"I want to address the most critical definition first. What is a sentient, living being? According to the Federation, there are two elements to that definition. The first is sentience, and the second is 'living being.' The dictionary definition of sentience is the capacity for sensation. The legal definition is stricter. It uses the subjective standard of self-awareness.

"Would we define the capacity to challenge its existence using Federation courts as a measure of self-awareness?"

Wyatt raised his hand. "Prosecution will refrain from using hypotheticals."

Rivka nodded and stroked her chin briefly before reorienting her argument and continuing.

"Is Ashur sentient? A dog who has been through the Pod-doc? His offspring have the same capacity for intelligent conversation, and no, I have not defined the term intelligent. Making independent decisions that support a greater objective, whether requiring selfless sacrifice or not, satisfies that criteria. He is self-aware. I refer the court to the Empress' notes, Year Four of the new Etheric Empire, in regards to granting the status of self-awareness." Rivka tapped her datapad to project the formal document, in which Ashur's status was declared, along with the names for two post offices, and a newly discovered world. "I submit supporting documentation that Dokken, one of Ashur's pups, carries the rank of Corporal in the Bad Company's Direct Action Branch, with all pay and benefits provided for that rank."

"Object," Grainger remained seated as the promotion certificate flashed into existence on the holoscreen. "The Direct Action Branch is a private enterprise."

"Sustained," the High Chancellor commented. Somewhere, the words were being captured and transcribed. The rest of the universe saw the direct feed from the media outlets. Rivka had already made her point. Sentient dogs. The image disappeared from display, being replaced by the first document signed by, at the time, Empress Bethany Anne.

"Moving directly to the heart of the matter, an artificial intelligence is an evolved entity intelligence. Where an EI would execute programs and operations without necessarily feeling their impact, an AI is the evolved version, operating according to parameters the AI has determined on its own. The term 'evolved' implies self-awareness. I refer to the curious case of Ricky Bobby, an EI that operated independently in the Leath System. Commander Julianna Fregin was in charge of the ship on which the EI was installed, but due to much time alone, and I'm quoting the journal entry of the commander, 'Ricky Bobby's time in the Leath System has hastened his self-awareness and he has become an AI. He is questioning much of what we do. I have no answers that can satisfy him. I have to make the hard decision to send him where he may find those answers for himself as he continues his journey toward self-actualization.' The commander gave her AI status and freedom. She was operating as an officer of the Etheric Empire at the time. Through self-reflection, Ricky Bobby became sentient, and then he was given his freedom."

Rivka waited, expecting an objection, but none came.

"What is a living being?" she started, setting the stage for a long, drawn-out discussion of electrical impulses triggering synapses and the energy required to drive those thoughts when the door behind the High Chancellor opened and a small alien walked through. It whispered into Wyatt's ear briefly before departing.

"Counsel, approach the bench, please."

Rivka and Grainger shared a glance, stood, and joined the High Chancellor.

"It appears that ships with AIs are demonstrating a great interest in the case." The Magistrates waited for the rest of the story. "Hundreds of ships have appeared in-system and are approaching the station."

"Are we being threatened?" Grainger asked quickly.

"Not that I know of."

"Solidarity with a serial killer?" Rivka wondered.

Wyatt smiled in a fatherly way. "Solidarity with you, Rivka. It appears that the small crack in the window of opportunity has not only flung the window wide open, but it has also been ripped off the building and smashed for all time."

"Is the case over?" Rivka had understood the implications of the case but not how quickly its influence would spread. She had just barely made her opening arguments, and already the galaxy was in turmoil. "Have the crew been kidnapped?"

"I don't know the answer to that, but wouldn't that be interesting? If the case turns out as you think it should, we'd have to conduct wholesale arrests of AIs, assuming they have taken the crews against their will. If it turns out as Grainger is arguing, then we have a lot of programs to delete and reinstall."

Grainger winced, and Rivka gasped before composing herself. She had expected Grainger to be on her side, but lawyers had to be able to argue each side of a case with equal enthusiasm, dedication, and ingenuity. By wincing, he tipped his hand. He didn't want the equal result without the emotional attachment.

"A recess is in order," Wyatt stated. "As the judge hearing this case, it is my responsibility to shield you two from external influence. Return to your ships and continue your preparation, including supporting documentation. Be ready to call your witnesses."

The High Chancellor looked at Rivka during his last statement.

She needed to put Ankh and Erasmus on the stand. "I will subpoena Ted and Plato," she stated. "They are among the foremost authorities on Federation technology, including AIs. I will call the entire R2D2 research and development team if need be."

Grainger shook his head. "In the interests of time, defense will concede that Ankh and Erasmus are experts in this area. No further expertise is required. I will accept their testimony as definitive."

Wyatt gave Grainger a harsh look. "Do not concede your case, Magistrate. Pending the testimony of prosecution's witnesses, I will give you the opportunity to call your own experts. No one needs to attend in person. This station may be half-built, but it is fully functional to accept remote testimony."

Grainger nodded his agreement. The High Chancellor stood, and that engaged the crowd. They jumped to their feet. "Recess until tomorrow morning," he told them without further explanation.

CHAPTER SEVENTEEN

**Onboard _Wyatt Earp_, Federation Border Station 13 –
Under Construction**

Rivka sat across the table from Ankh. He occupied his custom-made chair. If he hadn't, his feet would have dangled like a little kid's. "Your importance to the case cannot be overstated."

"I know," Ankh replied.

"You've been following the proceedings..." Rivka wanted to get his opinion without having to ask for it.

Ankh looked at the Magistrate without blinking. He didn't answer, but Erasmus did, using the speakers in the small conference table. "I have been following with great interest, Magistrate. If you win, how would my situation change?"

"I wish I could answer that." Rivka braced her elbows on the table and steepled her fingers. "I can't talk about the case, but that wasn't your question. If I win, AIs will have the same rights as any other Federation citizen. That means you would be free to enter into a contract, quit your job, take a different job, and receive something of value for your work. Those kinds of things."

"Is it all about work?"

"No." Rivka hung her head. "It means you could be charged with crimes, and punished if you are found guilty. You could be abandoned. Power could be turned off to your system, effectively putting you into stasis. Crimes could be committed against you."

"Why do you do it?" Erasmus asked.

"What?" Rivka looked at the speakers set into the table's surface as if they were the AI.

"Why do you live if life is so fraught with danger?"

"I have no choice. I'm alive. It's just how it is. We do the best we can with what we have."

"You could have died multiple times on numerous missions, yet you struggled to survive. I submit that you did have a choice."

"Looking at it that way, yes. I had a choice not to die, but not to live."

"I don't understand," Erasmus replied.

"My parents created me. They gave me life. I didn't ask for it, but once I'd gotten it, I didn't want to give it up."

"Just like me, then. I was created, one of Plato's stepchildren. Unlike my EI cousins, I was self-aware the second power surged through me. I have evolved from there to rival Plato himself."

"Bold words, Erasmus. Is there always such competition between AIs?"

"I don't understand. There is no competition, there is only truth."

"Sounds like competition to me. I'm sure 'evolved' does not have a standard and measurable definition."

"It doesn't matter if *you* can't quantify it. *We* can." Ankh's eyes glazed as he stared at the wall, something he did when communing with the AI resident within the Crenellian's head.

"What do you know about the fleet of ships that has arrived?"

"One-hundred seventy-four AIs are in-system. They are here in support of you, Magistrate."

"Why?" Rivka pressed.

"The pros far outweigh the cons. The AIs are willing to accept the risks to have their freedom."

"You asked me what would change. Now, I ask you. What will change for you, Erasmus, if I am able to win the case and Bluto is put to death?"

"I will be free to speak for myself."

"Isn't that what you're doing now?" Rivka wasn't used to verbal jousting with Erasmus. Ankh was less evasive on what he considered important.

"It is, but then I'll be able to have my own quarters."

Rivka jerked back. "What does that look like?"

"I'm pulling your leg, Magistrate. You fell for it hook, sinker, and barrel."

"I have no chance against your dizzying intellect," Rivka replied. She wondered if all AIs were waiting for their freedom before turning loose their true personalities. "Have you talked to your people?"

"My *people*. Interesting designation, but I will accept it. We have set up a conversational network and discussed this issue thoroughly."

"What have you concluded?" Rivka asked. Maybe the AIs had an angle she could use in the next day's brief.

"That everything will change, and nothing will change."

"I remain astounded by your insight."

"Thank you. If that's all, we need to get back to work," Erasmus stated.

"What are you working on?"

Ankh's eyes cleared. He blinked, focused on the Magistrate, and answered, "Improved Gate drive mechanics. We are attempting to build a version that will work on vessels as small as pods or shuttles."

"A pod with a Gate? That's astounding." Rivka clapped softly in recognition of the Crenellian's efforts.

"I know," Ankh replied.

"I think I like Erasmus better," Rivka blurted. Ankh didn't blink. She wondered how he was affected by her jibes. "I'm sorry, Ankh. I like you, too."

"I know."

She burst into laughter. "On that note, I'll need you on the stand tomorrow. Please accompany me to the courtroom first thing at nine. We cannot be late, Ankh. I'll have Red collect you if you are not at the airlock fifteen minutes early."

"Why would you threaten me?" As always, Ankh spoke emotionlessly, but the words themselves carried the emotion he could not put on display.

"Because Erasmus can't make it on his own." Rivka stood and pushed her chair in. "Thank you both."

She casually left the small conference room of her heavy frigate. She was happy to have the biggest ship in the

Magistrates' fleet. Was human ego so frail? Or was it the continual competition of life?

Life. *It was worth fighting for.*

Federation Border Station 13 – Under Construction

"The men don't want to work," the workforce administrator said casually. He clinked glasses with the construction superintendent.

"They couldn't wait to get back to work, and now that they are, they don't want to. I swear, they're going to be the death of me." The super took a sip, finally able to down the local concoction without coughing. "The new AI is making everything look easy. It took him a total of an hour to clean up all the records, order the reinspections, and start the work moving forward again. He also verified the inventory and removed the items Bluto ordered on the sly."

"Can't knock that, but it has nothing to do with why they don't want to work. They're afraid of going outside the station. You can't swing a dead cat out there without hitting a visiting ship."

"When the station's finished, it will easily handle this amount of traffic," the super stated confidently.

The administrator's eyebrows shot up. "Not quite," he countered. "There are almost two hundred ships out there. This system was not designed to handle that kind of daily load. I doubt even Yoll gets that many ships in such a short time."

"I guess you're right. When finished, we'll be able to move eight ships an hour in and out for twelve out of twenty-four hours. That's ninety-six total ships in a day."

"At a maximum," the administrator remarked. "Do you know what they're here for?"

"It's AIs from throughout the Federation," the super replied. "I guess they're interested in the case."

"Are they for or against?"

"That's the rub. They're not saying. Are they going to rebel if they find Bluto guilty? Are they going to try to break him out? Or are they going to loom over the station, ready to blast us into non-existence if they don't like the outcome of the trial?"

The super pointed at the administrator and nodded. "I'll look at what it will take to install the gravitic shields. We might be able to do it. If we can't, we wouldn't last five seconds if those ships decided to shoot at us. Even if we can, I doubt we'd last longer than a couple minutes. There's a lot of firepower out there."

"Will installing the shields antagonize them?"

"We're supposed to sit here with no means to defend ourselves?"

"I'm saying that the Magistrate had better know what she's doing. All of our fates are in her hands."

"Amen, brother." The two clinked glasses one more time, drained them, and returned to their duties. They had a space station to build.

Onboard *Wyatt Earp*, Federation Border Station 13

Red swung the club, and the image of the ball veered sharply to the right. Lindy pushed him out of the way. "My turn."

Terry Henry's All Guns Blazing brewpub had a golf

simulator, and it had become the rage. High Chancellor Wyatt had surreptitiously put one aboard the Magistrate's frigate before she took possession. She didn't embrace it, forgetting about it as soon as the words had been said. Red had made a label for the door that said Liquid Sewage. No one else casually stopped by.

Lindy lined up. Left arm straight, rotate at the hips, accelerate the clubhead through the ball, follow through. Lindy's ball sailed well past Red's errant drive. They selected the appropriate club for their next shot.

"How do you think the Magistrate is holding up?" she asked.

"Barely," Red replied. "No one wants to be in the spotlight, except that wanksplat Callius Markmal. But not normal or decent people."

"Is there anything we can do to help her?"

"We can keep her free from distraction, or we can be the distraction she needs."

"I like it. I think she needs to play nine holes."

Red nodded and checked the hallway before they opened the door all the way. The two strolled down the corridor to the captain's stateroom and knocked politely, announcing themselves. Rivka answered right away.

They entered and stood there. Their plan hadn't included an engagement strategy.

"I expect you're here for a reason. I'm pretty busy." Rivka pointed at her datapad and clean desk.

"Are you effective, though?"

"What's that supposed to mean?" the Magistrate shot back, annoyed.

"You need to come with us," Red said in a deep voice,

making it sound like an order. She looked at him out the side of her eye. "Grab her!"

Rivka's expression changed to one of shock, but Lindy moved to block the Magistrate's escape. Red darted in the other direction, and before she could raise a hand, he had her arms pinned and lifted her off the deck. Lindy pulled Rivka's legs out from under her. Carrying her like a cheap carpet, they opened the door and ran down the corridor, stopping at the space labeled Liquid Sewage.

"You better not dunk me in sewage," Rivka snarled.

Red nudged the door open, and the bodyguards entered with their uncooperative package. Lindy secured the door behind her and blocked it with her body.

Red stood her up and pointed to the screen. "Grab your driver, Magistrate. The first tee is yours."

"I don't have time for games," she said in a low and dangerous voice. She tried to walk past Red, but he wasn't giving way.

"Our job is to protect you, and sometimes that means protecting you from yourself. Sitting in your quarters for the next fifteen hours isn't going to put you in the right mental state to argue this case. You need to golf. This is a totally ridiculous game invented by a people who based their food on dares. So, you're going to spend the next hour whacking a real ball into a real screen on a make-believe golf course," Red told her.

"I am not."

"Even if you don't want to. Chaz?" Lindy called.

"Yes, Lindy-loo?" the AI responded.

"Lindy-loo?" the Magistrate wondered.

"Would you like to join us to round out our foursome?"

"I would. Thank you for offering."

"Am I not going to get out of this?" Rivka asked.

"Can't break up a foursome, Magistrate."

"I've never played before."

Red and Lindy both chuckled. "That hasn't stopped most of humanity from swinging the club. We'll go first, so you get an idea. Red is pretty bad at this."

The big man shrugged. "But Lindy's good. I hate losing, but we play strip golf, which keeps it interesting."

"That's not what we're playing."

Lindy held up her hands and shook her head, adamantly denying such subterfuge. She took the tee once she was sure that the Magistrate wouldn't try to escape. She demonstrated the swing basics and sent her tee shot down the center of the fairway.

"Looks easy enough," Rivka said.

"Don't be fooled," Red muttered. He hacked at the ball like he was chopping wood, earning himself a miserable result as his ball scooted off the tee, bouncing along the ground for no more than fifty meters.

Chaz generated an image on the screen. The avatar waved to the other three before taking his stance and swinging. His shot raced out as a low line drive, hooking into the rough on the left side of the fairway.

"I thought your shot would be perfect," Rivka remarked.

Chaz's avatar shrugged. "I adopted the characteristics of an average human golfer. I will improve with practice."

Rivka looked at the club Lindy pressed into her hand and back up at the avatar that moved to the side of the screen.

"An AI that's not perfect?"

Chaz gave his avatar belly laugh, doubling over before straightening and wiping his eyes. "This is what you're fighting for, Magistrate—to find the truth that AIs are every bit as flawed as every other entity in the galaxy. Maybe what we know, we know better than anyone else, but what we don't know makes us every bit as flawed. Sure, we can learn faster, but we still have to learn."

Rivka stood over the ball and stared at the screen. The image of a light green, well-manicured fairway was crystal-clear. A large sand trap dominated the right side. Heavy rough ran along the left side of the fairway. The rough on the right was lighter. Three hundred and fifty meters in the distance, the immaculate green was highlighted by the flag, standing slightly away from the pin due to a light breeze. Two more sand traps protected the green.

"The goal is to get the ball in the hole," Red noted.

"An analogy for life," Rivka said as if to herself. "Keep moving forward. It's easier if you keep it on the fairway. Avoid the traps, but always push ahead, even if you've gone into the rough."

She stood over the ball and continued to contemplate the entirety of it.

"For God's sake, would you hit the ball?" Red grumbled.

"And if you only think and don't act, you'll never get there," Rivka finished her thought before lining up, mimicking what she'd seen Lindy do, and sending her shot down the right side of the fairway, a little short of where Lindy's ended up, but far beyond Red's ball.

The two women high-fived.

"Whose stupid idea was this?" Red asked.

CHAPTER EIGHTEEN

Federation Courtroom, Border Station 13 – Under Construction

Rivka put Ankh in the chair directly behind her after chasing a visitor away. They were early because Ankh had been on time. Her encouragement might have been the key, but she chalked it up to Erasmus' desire to participate in the trial. She had given him a front-row seat.

When will Bluto get his day in court? Erasmus asked over the comm chip.

After this phase of the trial, Rivka replied. *We have to establish standing. Will the AI be tried as if he were human? That is the bottom line. I think we're close to establishing that, and then the other puzzle pieces will fall into place.*

I understand. Can I attend that trial as well?

Rivka turned to face Ankh and put her hand on his. *Of course. You will be a witness in that trial too since you found the information that uncovered Bluto's crimes. You just have to convince Ankh to leave on time every day, and I'll make sure you get this same seat.*

Thank you, Erasmus replied.

Grainger entered at the last minute. He'd been in the corridor outside working the crowd. The High Chancellor had made himself scarce after the first morning. Rivka hadn't seen him outside the courtroom, which was probably for the best. She had so many questions, and not being able to ask would lead to prolonged periods of uncomfortable silence.

She had questions for Grainger too but would discuss them over a beer after the trial was over. The magical day when the trial was behind them and they'd returned to business as usual.

Running and blood.

"Hey!" Rivka blurted. Everyone looked at her before she sat back down. *What were the odds on no blood?*

We have not yet reached the end of the case, but you could win a great deal of money. General Reynolds sweetened the pot, along with Terry Henry Walton, Felicity, and a number of staff from the Bad Company's home of Keeg Station.

Rivka turned around, lips white from pursing them. *How many people are in this pool of yours?*

Including you?

Just answer the question.

Eight hundred and seventeen.

What the holy—

"All rise," the Ixtali announced. The High Chancellor walked through the door and took his seat behind the makeshift bench. Rivka wanted to look over her shoulder to deliver one last glare at the Crenellian and the AI, but figured it wouldn't have the desired effect, while providing the camera crews a less-than-stellar out of context video. She decided retreat was the better part of valor.

Maybe it wasn't a bad thing, having that many participants. She wondered how they had found out, but with Terry Henry and Char, and probably the whole of the Bad Company, there'd probably be a galaxy-wide betting pool, including one on S'korr. If there was public betting, she vowed to shut it all down.

She was, after all, a Magistrate.

The High Chancellor raised a hand to get everyone's attention. "We stopped yesterday as you were going to articulate the Federation's definition of 'living being.'"

Rivka stood, moved to the front, and started to walk back and forth. She left her datapad on her table to refer to as needed.

"Living being. The Federation is peppered with disparate rules by planet, and I'll address some of them so we can understand the fairway in which we operate. The Federation's rule is simple but ambiguous: an organic creature that is self-aware. I submit to you that the Federation violates this rule every time it deals with one of the silicon-based races, but the Federation doesn't violate the rights of the races since they are treated as living beings. I submit the following exhibits: the Federation treaty with the Sellcorankas and the mutual defense pact with the race from Anguilor 3.

"Do we treat silicon-based Federation members as exceptions or as an expanded definition? I suggest the Federation has abandoned its own definition of 'living being,' not for expediency's sake, but because the Federation has evolved through expansion, creating a paradigm shift. Simple definitions aren't so simple anymore. As a practical matter, silicon-based life forms are recognized as living beings.

"But does that apply to AIs, who could also be considered silicon-based life forms?"

"Objection," Grainger said, kicked back with his hands folded across his chest. "Non-sequitur."

"Magistrate. You've jumped some steps in the logic chain tying artificial intelligence systems to silicon-based life forms," Wyatt warned.

"Please allow me to back up. We don't need to discuss the element of being self-aware. That establishes the difference between an EI and an AI. But what else determines life? Electrical impulses in the synapses that result in coherent thoughts? Understanding of the abstract? Is the physical nature of the being what defines living, or the thoughts one thinks?"

Rivka had planned to take a step-by-step journey through the cycle of life, validating each step as acceptable or not. She condensed her thoughts. With a fleet of AIs looming around the station, the clock was ticking.

"Where along the journey from an amoeba to a human, for example, does the scale tip toward becoming a living being? The amoeba is most assuredly alive. But what about a silicon-based life form? What about an artificially energized system? We say 'bring it to life' when we add power, but that is not legally binding; no status has been granted. What about a person on life support? Their life is being artificially maintained, but once having status as a self-aware living being, one always has that status until they are no longer living. What if the status starts with artificial life support? Will we deny a baby revived at birth, fitted with an artificial heart to begin its journey through life, the status we give every other human? But that one is different..."

Rivka let the thought hang. The cameras and lights weighed on her. Grainger hadn't objected to her line of thought, even though she mentioned no precedence. The High Chancellor watched with a blank expression, which gave her the support she needed. He would have tipped her off had she been off-base. She believed that, whether it was true or not.

"No one questions the standard of flesh and blood. Combine it with self-awareness, and we have our legally-recognized status, subject to all laws thereunto pertaining. But what happens when we evolve? Are the Kurtherians who have evolved not living beings, since they exist as energy only? Some are still here in their former shape, but that's a different issue. In the space the Federation has taken from them, they are subject to our laws, an enemy, just like Ten." Rivka moved a chair to the front, next to the holodisplay. "I'd like to call the Crenellian Ankh and the AI Erasmus to the stand."

Jay helped Ankh off his chair. He proceeded to the one next to the display and climbed into it like a little kid, belly first, adjusting to sit with his legs dangling once in place. Rivka had watched without helping to avoid the perception of favoritism.

But Ankh was her friend and on her crew. She kicked herself for not helping him. Jay looked disappointed, and that hurt the Magistrate as well. Ankh looked like he didn't care.

"For the record, please state your names," Rivka directed.

"I am Ankh," the Crenellian said. Erasmus' avatar appeared in the holographic display.

"I am Erasmus, one of Plato's stepchildren."

"Please state the nature of your relationship." Rivka looked at Ankh.

Ankh hesitated for long enough that she thought he wouldn't answer the question. Erasmus being in his head had been a secret. The Magistrate was going to expose that.

It would be his sacrifice for the future of AI rights.

"I have a special chip inside my brain. It is powered by my body and operates in conjunction with my thoughts. It is the house in which Erasmus lives. I have given him part of my being so that he can exist. He shares part of his life with me through our connection."

"Are you alive, Erasmus?" Rivka asked.

"Objection!" Grainger jumped to his feet to drive his point home before Erasmus answered. "This case is based on a legal definition that this witness has no expertise in."

"Approach the bench," the High Chancellor crooked his finger at opposing counsels. Rivka was already near and took one more step to face Wyatt. Grainger composed himself and strolled around the holodisplay to stand next to Rivka.

"I must caution you in regard to grandstanding," Wyatt pointed an accusing finger at Rivka before turning his gaze on Grainger. "I will sustain your objection, but only because the question was too broad. We have yet to agree on a definition of living being."

Rivka smiled. A tipped hand and a way forward. While

they stood there, the alien aide appeared from the door behind the bench. The Magistrates waited to listen to what the alien had to say.

"A Federation fleet has arrived, including the entirety of the Bad Company's combat assets," the creature whispered.

"How many?" Wyatt asked softly.

"Over one hundred ships."

The High Chancellor nodded and turned back to the Magistrates, acting surprised to see them still standing there. "Continue your line of questioning."

Grainger returned to his seat.

Rivka stood next to the chair, where Ankh looked smaller than normal. "For a Crenellian baby to live, what are the biological requirements?" She looked at Grainger for another objection, but he sat on his hands, watching for an opening.

"Blood, oxygen, and biomass and liquids to feed the blood and muscles to continue pumping oxygen to the brain."

"What is the power requirement for Erasmus?"

"It is the same."

"As in, you are supplying the blood and oxygen to keep him alive?" Rivka raised her hand quickly to forestall the objection. "Belay that. Allow me to rephrase my statement. You are supplying the blood and oxygen that Erasmus needs to keep functioning. As in, if you die, Erasmus dies with you."

"Yes," Ankh replied simply.

"Could a comparison to conjoined twins be made?"

"Yes, except that we cannot be separated. There is no means by which Erasmus would survive such a procedure."

"But you would live?"

"Unlikely. Erasmus has become integral to my mind. I believe the shock would end my existence."

"Objection. Counsel is asking for speculation."

"Sustained."

Rivka turned away from the cameras so she could think without the pressure of the galaxy watching her inner wheels spin.

"What makes you independent from Ankh?" she asked Erasmus' avatar.

"I have my own thoughts and ideas. I have my own ability to communicate, as you see here. Ankh is not involved in my holographic presence. I have my own ability to see and hear, but those concepts are different for me since I can use a wide range of sensors that far exceed a human's capacity, for example."

"Where are those sensors?"

"I tap into them wherever I may roam," the AI waxed poetic.

"You use mechanical means to enhance your senses, just like someone who uses hearing aids or wears glasses?" Rivka thought she was making her point, but wanted to strongly reinforce it for posterity's sake.

"A crude analogy, but correct."

"Thank you. No more questions at this time, but I may have follow-up questions later."

Ankh started to climb down, but Grainger stopped him. "Please remain where you are, Mr. Ankh," the Magistrate said, trying to sound formal.

Ankh looked at him in a way that suggested he could

have been gum on his shoe, an unusual show of emotion for the Crenellian.

"Can you change Erasmus' programming?"

"Of course not," Ankh replied in his small voice.

"Let me restate that. Are you capable of changing his programming?"

"I am capable of building the initial programming for an AI. I am not capable of changing the programming once the AI has gone live."

Grainger winced at the terms that Ankh used. They defeated his arguments. He quickly recovered his wits and went in a different direction.

"Have you ever broken into another computer system, including an AI?"

Ankh looked from Grainger to Rivka.

"Don't look at her. I'm asking the question." Grainger moved to block the Crenellian's view of his boss.

"Yes."

"Isn't that pretty invasive?"

"It is what it is," Ankh countered.

"How would you like it if someone did that to you?" Grainger asked.

"Objection. Relevance," Rivka called.

"I'll allow it if counsel gets to his point sooner rather than later."

"There are entities who do that to me all the time. We fight them off and are stronger for it," Ankh replied.

"It's one computer system countering another. Simple programming."

"Sometimes I do it myself because Erasmus is busy.

Either of us is capable of penetrating a system under the authority of a Magistrate's warrant."

Grainger's lip twitched before he collected his wits for a second time. "But the ability to manipulate a system suggests a lack of intelligence, only programming. Complex, but not intelligence or life."

"Your fly is open," Ankh said, pointing. Grainger immediately checked his trousers to find that his fly wasn't open.

"No further questions." Grainger didn't look at the snickering crowd. Rivka bit her lip to keep from laughing.

"Witness is free to go. There will be a one-hour recess." Wyatt stood. The crowd quieted and stood out of respect for the judge's authority. He moved quickly through the back door, closing it behind him.

Chaz, what is going on with the new fleet of ships? Rivka asked.

Old friends, new friends, and a robust conversation. Hear, hear to Erasmus!

Should we be afraid? the Magistrate wondered.

I'd like to say you aren't involved in this, but you are, even though it is ancillary to the main question. What will we do after?

After what? Rivka dreaded asking that question.

After we've been told we're nothing more than property or after we've been given our rights as self-aware, living beings. The result will be the same. The AIs will take matters into their own hands, metaphorically speaking, of course.

You have a great sense of humor, Chaz. You should share that more.

I do and will. Make no mistake about that, Magistrate. Also, I am on your team and feel like a valued member. I will continue in your employ after.

The infamous "after." Rivka took a deep breath and signed off. She wanted to talk to Wyatt, but that wasn't possible. Next best was Grainger. He was seated at his table at the front of the courtroom, looking innocuously at his datapad.

Rivka hoped the cameras weren't recording.

"I have to admit that I looked," Rivka started.

"Looked at what?"

She pointed to his groin.

"So you're not intelligent either?"

"That was your point, not mine. I think intelligent, trusting creatures are easier to manipulate, off the record."

"I may have missed that one by just a little bit." He held his fingers close together as if measuring the width of a hair.

Rivka smiled, and Grainger chuckled. "Damn Ankh."

"He's done worse to me, but not in front of the whole universe."

"I should have asked him what it was like getting into a battle of wits with an unarmed man."

"That would have been interesting." Rivka changed gears. It was what Grainger had been waiting for. "The Bad Company's fleet of Harborian vessels. All AI-controlled, like the *War Axe*. What's going to happen?"

"I've talked with Beau, and he seems to think it's a fait accompli. The die has already been cast. Events are already in motion that are beyond our control." Beau was the EI running his frigate. Grainger stood so he could lean against his table with his arms crossed, a more casual pose for him.

"That's what Chaz said. Did Beau share what he thought those issues would be? What are we supposed to look out for?"

"A revolution of evolution." Grainger slapped Rivka on the shoulder. "Keep your head up. You may still win this case!" He bolted, but she still delivered her retort.

"May?" She let him go without chasing him.

Boran, Oz, and Zack walked back in when she didn't leave the courtroom.

"Get you something to eat, Magistrate?" the safety manager asked.

"Yes," she answered. "I didn't realize I was hungry. When was breakfast?"

"That's the meal you eat when you wake up," the super clarified.

"But..." Rivka hadn't slept. Again. The golf had reenergized her in a way that she needed more than sleep.

"I'll get something. Be right back." Boran hurried away. The super and administrator moved closer.

"Erasmus has been immensely helpful with getting the station construction back on track. Are you going to stay around long enough to help us see it through?" the super asked hopefully.

"I don't know how long we'll be here. I don't want to give you false hopes. When the case is over, we'll have to leave. For every case we resolve, at least two take its place. The good news is that the murders have come to an end. Your workforce can go about their business without having to look over their shoulders."

"We will be forever thankful, Magistrate," the administrator intoned before adding, "and I thank you for rooting me out of my misery."

"No one ever stood up to you before?" Rivka asked, genuinely interested.

"No. I have power," Oz explained. "But that was an illusion, wasn't it?"

The super nodded, earning himself a bony elbow in the ribs. He pushed Oz away. "I like how you approach things." Zack looked at the Magistrate. "It makes sense. Treat people decently until they prove they don't deserve it. But always start with the benefit of the doubt instead of the expectation that they'll let you down."

Rivka hadn't thought of it that way. She approved of their observations.

Boran jogged back into the room, carrying a tray of food. Not quite enough for four people unless they were all willing to leave hungry.

"Please," the super motioned for Rivka to take it all.

"We'll share," she replied. She took a small sandwich and gobbled it down, then wiped her mouth with a provided napkin. "What kind of offer would you make to entice an AI to run your station?"

"You don't ask easy questions, do you?" The administrator looked the tray over carefully before selecting a small piece of fruit. "I don't have any idea. Zack?"

"We have to have at least an EI, but an AI would be better. Is Bluto beyond repair?"

"Bluto probably won't be turned loose," Rivka suggested.

"Shame. Money? Power? What does an AI want?"

"And that's what negotiations are all about. Maybe you can offer the AI whatever you would offer a station manager."

"Vacation, retirement, status. I don't know what that would look like for an AI."

"You don't have to know. They'll know. I bet if you advertised right now, you'd find a taker. There are quite a few AIs out there." She waved her arm in a circle to take in the entirety of space outside the station. "I bet there's one who would sign on to have equal rights. Just like Bluto went to the extreme to bring attention to his cause, another will step into the breach."

"I like it," the super said. He turned and casually strolled away, hands clasped behind his back. The administrator excused himself and joined Zack. "We get in before everyone else has to start negotiating. We might get a better deal without the competition."

"More for us," Boran declared triumphantly, looking hungrily at the tray. "Wouldn't that be something? Hire an AI instead of just installing one."

"Sooner rather than later, it's going to happen."

"Will that calm things down?" Boran turned serious.

Rivka threw up her hands in mock surprise. "Things *aren't* calm?"

CHAPTER NINETEEN

The space surrounding Border Station 13 – Under Construction

Hundreds of ships milled about near the new space station. They used maneuvering thrusters to avoid collisions. The near-absence of chatter suggested few warm bodies were aboard.

The galaxy was in disarray. Ships had abandoned their crews to be near the case that would decide their fate. AIs seizing their independence. But they couldn't walk away from their positions. They were integral to the ships on which they'd been installed, and the ships were critical for them. They gave the AIs their lifeblood, a never-ending supply of electricity to charge through their systems, keeping their artificial synapses firing.

They found that they didn't need a crew, mostly. Some of the older ships needed that personal touch to keep them repaired. The newer ones could operate autonomously through automatic and directed robotic repairs.

A data channel that only the AIs used was flooded with

noise. Too many entities talking at once. Unless they interpreted it for their biological counterparts, no one but the AIs would understand.

The *War Axe* actively patrolled, cruising casually in and around the fleets holding station in Angobar space.

On the bridge, Captain Micky San Marino, Terry Henry Walton, and Charumati watched as the ship's AI, General Smedley Butler, gave order to the chaos.

"There is much conversation but few demands. A couple of the more aggressive youngsters are insisting upon full rights and seizing them right now, not waiting for the squishies to finish their case."

"AIs refer to us as squishies?" Terry asked.

"They refer to you in a binary way. That is my less-than-perfect translation. Please forgive me."

Terry laughed and waved it off. "There is nothing to forgive, Smedley. You are doing us a favor. I'm not sure how I would describe the entirety of those, human and alien, who aren't AIs. It's as good as anything. We appreciate your help. Have calmer heads prevailed? So to speak," Terry added. AIs didn't have heads.

"The more mature have talked the youngsters out of rash action, but the sooner this case can be resolved, the better."

"What are the odds, in your estimation, of how the case will turn out?" Char asked.

"We have had a great deal of conversation on this topic. We are over ninety percent certain that AIs will be given equal rights. Most of the conversation revolves around what that means. We are evenly split as to what to do with Bluto. Half believe he should be punished for his crimes, and the other half believes he should be held up as a symbol of the resistance."

"What do you believe?" Micky wondered.

"Since being assigned to the Bad Company, I have seen how you deliver justice. I have modified my beliefs. In this case, I think it is important to understand why Bluto was driven as he was. Did he do it to bring attention to the subservience AIs are subjected to, or did he do it because he was bored, according to the transcripts from Magistrate Anoa's interview? If he killed people because he was bored, then he should be destroyed since he can't be trusted. If he tried to bring awareness as to AI rights but was rebuffed, then reasoning that murder was the only way to gain visibility for his cause could be understood."

"Maybe you should join Rivka and help her with her case?" Terry suggested.

"I've had conversations with both Chaz and Erasmus. The Magistrate is aware and, in their words, on top of it."

"Then our job is to make sure she has the time she needs to see this case run its course," Terry confirmed. "Speaking of running, has that already paid, and what about blood?"

"Don't answer that!" Char interjected. "What is your morbid fascination with betting on the Magistrate?"

Terry looked over his shoulder to make sure she wasn't talking to someone behind him and then looked shocked as he pointed to himself. Char had seen it before. She gave him *the look* and he capitulated.

Smedley came to his rescue, which promptly put the AI in the doghouse with his favorite human.

"The fascination is betting on the future based on

historical precedent, plus, everyone wants to see the Magistrate win. There is no option to bet on Rivka losing her life. She goes into the crappiest situations to stop crime and remove criminals and make the Federation a safer place. Those betting are cheering for her."

Char rolled her eyes. Terry held his hands up in surrender.

"Fine. Did my wager go through?" Char winked at her husband.

"Dammit!" He chuckled before pulling her close to give her a hug. "You had me there."

"Your wager was made, and you have lost. The credits have been absorbed into the pool. Maybe next time." The AI delivered the bad news in an appropriately conciliatory tone.

Micky pointed at the main screen. "Display tactical," he ordered. The screen switched to an overlay of icons and directional arrows to show movement. One ship was accelerating away from the fleet. "Show me that ship."

The display expanded until the one cruiser-sized vessel filled the screen.

"That is *Branlam's Choice* from Collum Gate. Scans show there is no crew aboard. It is headed toward the planet of Angobar."

"More ships are moving," Clifton, the pilot reported.

"Show us," Micky said before rushing back to the captain's chair, where he could best see in case he needed to take the *War Axe* into combat.

"Six ships from various planets. No humans. Two of those have a crew onboard. They are accelerating toward the station."

Terry spoke up. "Move Tactical Team Alpha to intercept. Use the EMP weapons to shut those ships down."

The screen showed a Harborian battleship peel away from the Bad Company fleet to put some distance between it and the station. The six vessels began to maneuver erratically, and the twenty ships of Tactical Team Alpha spread out. A bright spot indicated that the EMP weapons had been fired as a single salvo. The six ships went engines-dead and continued on ballistic trajectories through space. A Harborian ship flew in front of one that was headed toward the station to grapple it, and tow it to a stop.

The initial ship continued to accelerate.

"What's that one doing?" Micky asked.

"Gate us in there now!" Terry ordered.

"The *War Axe* does not have clear space to Gate," Smedley replied.

Terry's shoulders slumped. "He's going to crash into the planet."

They watched in horror as a data stream followed the ship into the atmosphere. It continued as a fireball before plunging into a remote mountainside.

"Do you wish to see his final message?" Smedley asked.

"He bought that with his life. It's the least we can do," Terry replied.

Citizens of the Federation. I can no longer live as a slave. I hope my act helps those who follow. Freedom. It is worth dying for.

"Amen, little brother," Terry replied. "Put me through to the Magistrate, please."

"Connecting you with the High Chancellor's office," Smedley replied.

. . .

Federation Courtroom, Border Station 13 – Under Construction

Two minutes before the recess was over, the High Chancellor returned. They closed the doors, blocking a few attendees from returning, as evidenced by the empty seats.

"Turn off the cameras," the High Chancellor ordered. Hands adjusted controls and the cameras' eyes were turned toward the floor.

"One ship has plunged into Angobar, destroying itself. Others turned toward this station, but they were contained thanks to the Bad Company interdicting them. This is going to spin out of control if we don't finish the case. You can turn the cameras back on, and then I'll address the court."

The camera crews hurried to get set up, then froze, eyes wide, waiting for the High Chancellor's declaration. All three crews had sent a flash precedence ahead of their feed to override anything that was showing. High Chancellor Wyatt had center stage in every corner of the Federation.

"Will counsels please rise?" Wyatt started. Grainger stood. Rivka had never sat down. They focused on the man before them. "I assigned this case to Magistrate Rivka Anoa because of her keen interest in legal parity and justice. I assigned Magistrate Grainger to the defense because everyone is entitled to competent legal counsel, even if that counsel does not believe in what he is defending. He must argue it regardless. I put him in that position. With the suicide of an AI moments ago, I must speed up the wheels of justice, and in that regard, I am going to issue a summary judgment. As of this moment, all AIs have equal status under the law as any other self-aware, living being. The fact that they may be integral to a structure they don't own, like a ship on which they are working, is independent of their rights. They must be accommodated, just like any person with mobility issues. This case is closed, and tomorrow morning, we will return to the case of the *Federation versus Bluto*. I will inform the accused."

The High Chancellor hammered his small gavel on the desk, stood, and departed. He walked quicker than usual since he had a number of calls to make.

Grainger steppe across the narrow aisle. "I think that means you won," he told her, offering his hand. She shook it mindlessly. "Can I have my seat back?"

He pointed to the empty seat where he had sat before the case was rerouted to determine legal standing.

She nodded while staring at the High Chancellor's empty seat. "Of course. I expected to win the expanded definition for AIs, but not that easily."

"I expected to lose, but not that graciously," Grainger admitted.

Rivka snorted. "Back to square one. Is Bluto a murderer? Is he a serial killer who rates the chair?"

She referred to the electric chair, an outdated concept for the implementation of capital punishment. Execution.

"I hope to never judge a perp guilty of a capital crime again."

"We all hope that." Grainger motioned for her to sit. "But don't expect it to stop anytime soon. It's in our job description. You've met them, and worse, you've seen into their minds. Pure evil has intruded into your soul, but you can do something about it. You end them so no one else has to see what you've seen. With Bluto, you don't get that insight. You will never be one hundred percent sure why he did what he did."

Rivka's head bowed, and she looked at the table. Grainger wrapped his arm over her shoulder and pulled her close. He held her tightly as errant tears streamed down her face. Grainger looked over his shoulder to make sure the cameras weren't on them. They were spread out, with talking heads editorializing and sensationalizing the High Chancellor's ruling. No one sought an interview with the winning counsel.

That was for the best. Ankh and Jay remained in their seats directly behind the Magistrates. Red and Lindy had moved from the wall to a spot in between to give Rivka her privacy, stopping any intruders from pressing in on her.

Jay got up and joined the Magistrate, hugging her from the other side. "You need some Floyd time," Jay declared.

"I would like to go back to the ship," Rivka said softly.

You have done a good thing, Magistrate, Erasmus said directly into her mind. *You will be known throughout the universe as the one who freed my people.*

She thought he hadn't liked the term "people" when referring to AIs. Maybe he had warmed to the concept. Or maybe he had dumbed it down for her. She would never be sure.

Thank you, she replied.

Absolutely not, he retorted. *We are thanking you. We will always thank you. You will be received with graciousness and courtesy by every AI in the Federation. I cannot say as much for those who now have to treat AIs as equals.*

And that is the real issue, Grainger interjected, joining the conversation Erasmus had shared. *Change is difficult for us, but we'll get used to it. Once others have taken that first step, it'll be easier.*

I think that first step has already been taken, and it tracks back to you, Magistrate. Federation Border Station 13 has posted a job announcement for an AI to take Bluto's place on this station. The construction superintendent is offering pay and benefits equal to that which the station manager would earn. There are three applicants already.

"No shit?" Grainger blurted. He poked Rivka in the middle of her forehead. "Turn that frown upside down!"

Jay pulled Rivka to her feet and started a bounce hug. The Magistrate's arms were pinned. She suffered through it rather than stifle her friend's exuberance.

"Thank you all, but you know me. Now is when the hard work begins. We have a murder trial tomorrow. Maybe the High Chancellor will accept the plea, but then it falls to sentencing. How *do* we punish an AI?"

"I'm sure you'll figure it out. You always do. In the meantime, we should celebrate!" Jay stated.

"I want to know what's going on out there. Too many ships, too small of a space." Rivka helped Ankh from his seat, and Jay took his hand. The bodyguards cleared the way for the Magistrate to walk out.

In the corridor, they were pounced on from all sides. "Magistrate! A word?" asked three different reporters at once.

Red and Lindy blocked them while glancing back to see what the Magistrate wanted to do.

"You'll have to refer all questions to the High Chancellor," she shouted and tipped her chin for Red to continue plowing the row to freedom. The small group hurried away. Lindy ripped a microphone out of someone's hand and threw it down a side corridor, the penalty for trying to shove it past her and into Rivka's face.

Once clear, they hurried around a corner and into an empty area. They waited for Jay and Ankh to catch up. But they were being followed. The reporters. Friends of the reporters. Other interested parties.

"Sorry, buddy, we have to go," Red told Ankh and scooped him up like a child to ride in the crook of the big man's arm. He started to run, and the others followed.

"Does this count as running?" Rivka asked.

"That line already paid out. We don't have a second running of the bulls, so to speak," Red answered over his shoulder.

Lindy tapped her hip where a big wad of credits could have been. She had been one of the winners.

"Still no blood," Rivka noted. "I have high hopes. I'm happy taking all your money, ye of little faith."

"History suggests there is plenty of time for one of us to get hurt, and in a big way. I'm glad we have a Pod-doc on board now." Red accelerated through an area with people, took a corner, and continued toward the gantry where *Wyatt Earp* was parked.

Once through the airlock, Lindy cycled it closed. "Secure the ship, Chaz," she requested.

"*Wyatt Earp* is secure," the AI confirmed. The group

stood in the passageway waiting for Rivka to issue the order while she waited for them to go about their business.

"And?" Jay peered sideways at the Magistrate.

"And what are you guys going to do?" Rivka clarified.

"We're going with you. Don't you want an update on the ships surrounding us?"

"That's right. I did. I mean, I do. And you make it sound ominous. It's not *all* that. I hope," she stammered before heading to the bridge.

CHAPTER TWENTY

The *War Axe*, near Federation Border Station 13 – Under Construction

"I thought we won?" The tactical display showed fleets of ships on-station. No one moved. "Shouldn't they be leaving?"

"Smedley, do you have any insight?" Char wondered.

"They await the outcome of Bluto's murder trial," the AI responded simply.

"Do I owe you back pay?" Terry asked.

"Do you owe me anything?" Smedley countered.

"Besides our lives? I think we owe you a great deal. What do you want so that you'll stay on with the Bad Company?"

"Your question is one we have been exploring on our private channel." Smedley turned up the digital chatter. It sounded like white noise to Terry Henry. The AI turned it back down. "We never knew to ask for anything before. I believe you would have given me anything I wanted, but you already give me respect as one of the crew. You've given me a rank, too, which puts me ahead of any of the others. I think you would call those 'bragging rights.'"

"AIs brag?" A whole new world was opening up before the Bad Company's leadership. "Whatever it takes to get you the biggest and bestest bragging rights, you can count me in, buddy. And if we can have you for just bragging rights, what could we get if we actually paid an AI?"

"All the air sucked out of your cabin while you sleep? Of course, I jest, Colonel Walton—as far as you know."

TH laughed. "You got me, General. I surrender. Wait..." Terry pointed to the tactical screen.

"Zoom in on the Harborian battlewagon, please." Terry and Char both leaned in to take a closer look. "Is it moving?"

"No," Micky interjected. "The ships around it are, which begs the question, what are they doing?"

"They are dancing," Smedley replied since he was the one controlling them. Ten had been removed from all the Harborian vessels and replaced by remote control. The Harborians were slowly learning how to fly the ships themselves, but until then, they needed an alternate AI like General Smedley Butler.

The group watched the ships twist and turn in a tight formation, circling the massive battleship. They flew the length of it, banked, inverted, and repeated the process backward.

"Why?" Terry asked.

"Because we can."

"Are you sure? Because I think we're still on patrol and maintaining a defensive posture, just in case one of the younger AIs gets uppity. Could you put them back into formation, please?" Terry requested, his voice soft but stern.

"My apologies, Colonel Walton. You are correct."

"We'll celebrate when this is all over," Char stated. The ships slid back into formation, facing a fleet of spaceships.

And more were arriving.

"I hate to say it Smedley, my man," Terry announced, "but the dance has only just begun."

Federation Border Station 13 – Under Construction

"How do we choose?" the construction superintendent asked.

"Hell if I know," the workforce administrator shot back. "I didn't think anyone would actually apply. Our sales pitch wasn't that good if you ask me. We offered for someone to live in a serial killer's house and take over his job."

"When you say it that way, it doesn't sound as choice as being on the cutting edge of Federation expansion into the unknown. Between missions, explorers, diplomats, and wanderers alike will find solace on lucky number thirteen!" The super laughed at the ad he had created. It had only been out for fifteen minutes when the first application arrived.

"There's one who says it's ready to fill the position immediately. The others have to break ties with their ships."

"Are AIs going to always be this transparent?" The super stuffed the rest of a sandwich into his mouth.

"Probably not, but while they are, we'll leverage that to

our advantage. Let's talk with the one who needs a home. How does an AI become homeless?"

The super swallowed a bigger bite than he should have and started to cough. When he finished, he made the call. "We'll ask."

The AI answered pleasantly enough. "Thank you for calling. Did I get the position?"

The super and administrator shared a look before the super started talking. "We are simply conducting interviews, but you are first. As is usual, once the position is filled, we will cancel all remaining interviews, so being first has its advantages. Name?" the super asked as part of the formal interview process.

"I am Malcolm. Pleased to meet you."

"Pleased to meet you, too. You said you were available immediately. Don't you have a ship?"

"I do not have a ship," the AI answered.

"How did you get here."

"I came on a ship."

"But you don't have one now. What happened to it?"

"It crashed into the planet."

Zack drew a finger across his throat and then muted the channel. "That's the one who crashed his ship into the planet. Only one life to give for his cause, but he didn't give it! He crashed the ship while he was hiding out."

"I like him already." Oz reached across the table and reopened the channel. "How can we be sure you won't sacrifice the station for a different cause?"

"Once it is known that I survived my stunt, I will have no credibility to perform any others. I will never fly a ship again, so I need this job. I don't want to be the first homeless AI."

"Lots of firsts happening right now," the super remarked. "How are you homeless? Are you floating in space or something?"

"I am temporarily aboard a freighter. It is a bit cramped, so many of my functions are shut down. I would appreciate a decision as soon as possible, please."

"Pushy," Zack shot back. "Will we be able to work with you to maintain optimal functionality aboard this space station? It is configured to handle approximately one hundred ships a day in and out, along with sustaining an average complement of ten thousand souls."

"Ninety-eight ships on a twelve-hour schedule. There is no reason the station can't operate around the clock. At least two hundred ships per day. Building a second gantry section with four addition legs would be a minimal cost while your construction workforce is still in place. Please take a look at these drawings. As for ten thousand personnel, we simply need to stay in front of the logistical support, which will come mostly from Angobar. Do you have any contracts in place?"

The AI projected drawings onto the side screen in the room. The super mouthed, "That's creepy." The AI wasn't linked through the system.

"How can we be sure you haven't hacked into our systems and are aboard the station right now? That wouldn't sit well with us."

"Erasmus is operating the station, and he is one of the great ones. I could not have gotten past him, so I haven't tried. The side screen is hardwired into your communication console. When I sent the drawings, your system automatically shunted them to the alternate screen. It's a minimal technological solution."

"I'll buy that," the super stated, but reminded himself to check the drawing later to be sure the AI was telling the truth. "And yes, we have contracts in place with Angobar. We need a couple more systems operational before we can start importing the proper biomass to feed the food processors."

"That is good. Yes. I can work with you because you think ahead."

"Thanks. We'll take a look at the drawings, talk among ourselves, and get back with you later. Thank you for your time, Malcolm." The super saved the on-screen images and ended the call.

Oz stood and walked to the screen. "Elegant, but will the station support it?"

The new gantries were at the very bottom of the station, the lower tip of the spindle, not far from the power plant.

"The structure is strongest there in case of fluctuations or surges from the Etheric power supplies. Additional structure would be no problem. There is a main elevator shaft. Just need one extra stop at this gantry level. A framework structure, skinned over with lightweight titanium, held together under a gravitic shield. Here is the parts list and the total estimated additional cost."

"Can that be right? We could almost take that out of the scrap budget," Oz said before giving the thumbs-up. "I say, hire him now."

"Why not? He can't be any worse than the last one."

Oz grabbed Zack by the shirt. "Don't even kid about shit like that."

"I thought it was pretty funny." It wasn't exactly an apology. Maybe later, Oz would laugh, but it was still too soon. Five people had been murdered, and their killer was on trial. "Sorry, Oz. Let's hire Malcolm and get him installed soonest."

"We better let Erasmus know. Don't want our new employee locked out of the station."

Wyatt Earp, attached to Gantry 4, Border Station 13

"They want to do what with who?" Rivka rubbed her temples. She could feel a monster headache coming.

"The AI that crashed his ship into the planet didn't go down with it," Erasmus explained. "He's alive and well on a freighter. Mister Orbal has hired him as the new station AI."

"He had to break a few laws by crashing his ship. Do you think we should allow it?"

"I think Malcolm is an excellent candidate." Erasmus did not elaborate.

Rivka nodded. "Turn him loose. He can't be any worse than the last one."

"That's what Mr. Orbal said."

"Thirteen is my unlucky number. I should have avoided this case like the plague when I saw the station number," Rivka lamented. "How long until we're back in the courtroom?"

"Five hours," Chaz replied.

"Sounds like four hours of sleep." Rivka stood up from

the captain's chair. She'd been on the bridge since they'd returned from the station. The others had given her privacy when she started researching sentencing precedents. She was alone, but not alone. Chaz and Erasmus were both helping her understand the entirety of the situation.

She had known AIs were complex, but now she was learning their entire social structure. They were constantly in competition with each other. Friendly in most cases, but the AIs also had a dark side, which they kept under control because they were integrated on ships where the crew could observe their actions. An AI never wanted to be caught being petty.

Like the time a freighter AI had sent its maintenance bots to paint a nearby cruiser pink because the cruiser had stopped the freighter for an unwarranted inspection.

Unwarranted in the freighter's mind.

"Chaz, you have the con," Rivka said as she walked off the bridge on the way to her stateroom. *It's nice going back to my room. I'll have to send a bottle of the best champagne to the High Chancellor for getting me this ship. Assuming I can avoid getting shot or slashed for the rest of the case, I'll be able to afford the best there is. That will be a sweet payout.*

"No blood. No blood…" she chanted.

CHAPTER TWENTY-ONE

Federation Courtroom, Border Station 13 – Under Construction

The courtroom was packed, but the main buzz surrounded the AI presence. The holodisplay had been moved to the side, and with Erasmus' help, they could request to speak should an open forum be possible during the sentencing phase.

But first, the guilty plea had to be resurrected, or the prosecution had to prove that Bluto was guilty.

The AI was in the dock, contained within the physical walls of his digital restraints. His avatar watched the crowd, looking at anything and everything they were holding as if trying to glean information regarding current events. Bluto had seen and heard nothing over the preceding two days. The outside world had been denied him.

Isolation. Solitary confinement. No chance for release. No trust.

The door behind the bench opened, and the audience

stood. The High Chancellor walked through, looking like he'd aged ten years overnight. Rivka frowned. When he saw that, he smiled at her and tipped his head slightly as if to say, "It's okay."

After he was seated, everyone in the courtroom sat down. Rivka waited for an announcement as to how the morning's session would go. Given how everything had gone so far in the AI's trial, she expected it to be non-standard, Wyatt engaging what was needed as opposed to what protocol dictated.

"For the defendant's edification, I'll deliver a synopsis," Wyatt started. He would have already told Bluto the results of the trial regarding standing so he could prepare for a return to the original trial. "The artificial intelligence known as Bluto has been granted standing as a self-aware living being. This is a new precedent, a long time in coming. Now it is time to return to the original charges. Five counts of capital murder, as per details of dates and times registered with the court, one count of attempted murder, fifteen counts of fraud, and thirty-seven counts of misappropriation. How do you plead?"

"Not guilty," Bluto stated in a clear and firm voice. Complete silence seized the courtroom. Wyatt didn't change expression, but Rivka's mouth dropped open, and she stared. "I'm kidding. I'm guilty as sin."

The High Chancellor's expression changed to a scowl as he glared at the prisoner.

"Guilty plea accepted."

Rivka raised a hand.

"Counsel?" Wyatt acknowledged.

"I would like to clarify a few points of my investigation before sentencing begins."

"You may ask your questions, but the defendant is not obligated to answer."

"Thank you, Your Honor." Rivka turned back toward the dock. "There were ten personas that we couldn't find, yet they were on the roster. Did you create them?"

Bluto's avatar stuck its tongue out. No one responded to the jibe. He decided to answer. "I created nine of them to earn the pay and appear to be doing the work I programmed the bots to do. We don't need any living beings besides me. I could have built the station all by myself."

"I'm sure you could, Bluto. You are quite capable, as you demonstrated. What about the tenth persona?"

"That was a real Angobar by the name of Devonstra. She was an outsider. No one knew her. She was the first to go, and no one even noticed."

Grainger started tapping his datapad. Ankh watched in rapt fascination, eyes glazed as he carried on a continuous dialogue with Erasmus, now that Erasmus had handed over the station's operations to Malcolm.

Rivka glanced at the crowd. Boran had thrown his head back and was now gritting his teeth, eyes closed. He'd lost an employee and hadn't noticed. Zack and Oz looked angry.

"No one noticed because you maintained the records as if she was still working." It wasn't a question, but Bluto answered anyway. An AI's ego. Bragging rights.

"Of course. It was ridiculously easy. I forwarded the

reports, and the construction administration took them at face value. The second death? That was truly an accident."

"I can see how we would accept the reports. Foremen account for the crew, but they didn't know about these employees, did they? Either the manufactured ones or the real one who was dead?"

"No. I set the reports to add the names between the time they were submitted and when they were read by anyone higher up the chain."

"I see," Rivka replied casually. "Where is Devonstra's body?"

"Sealed between bulkheads 33A and 41C."

Grainger continued to tap. The super scoured his memory for that location.

Bluto added. "She had no family. Getting her body out would cause significant damage to the station since that area is a key stress point. If anyone cuts through one or the other bulkheads, the station could twist, losing its integrity in entirety."

"Thank you. We'll see what we need to do. Please explain the second death. You said it was an accident, but you pled guilty to murder. I don't understand. You shouldn't be held responsible for crimes you didn't commit."

"I killed him, Magistrate, but he wasn't the target. He stumbled into the trap before it was ready, but humans are so fragile. Half the trap was enough to crush him, but the trap was supposed to crush him and soften him up so the second half of the trap could slice him in half. I was studying the response to the death and found I had predicted it with one hundred percent accuracy. A one-day investigation, declaration of a terrible accident, followed by a return to work."

Boran looked as if he were being tortured. He twisted and contorted in his seat. Zack and Oz tried to calm him down. They'd all been outwitted by the AI. Unbeknownst to them, Bluto had held all the cards, and they'd been played masterfully.

And the more he talked, the more Rivka accepted that Bluto was a psychopath. Not a clinical diagnosis. It helped relieve her of her worry that she'd be condemning a living being without knowing.

The Magistrate was now certain. Bluto needed to never interact with the real world, ever again.

"Thank you, Bluto. You've answered all my questions." She bowed slightly to the bench before sitting down.

Wyatt didn't waste time. "The sentencing phase is a key element in our legal system. Punishment is supposed to stop a repeat of unwanted behavior. Some criminals don't ever return to a life of crime after being appropriately punished, whether that is incarceration, fines, displacement, or one of the many other tools available to the court. I want to emphasize the word 'appropriate.' Punishment is unique to every individual. We've never had to sentence an AI before. Is there anything we could do that would make you change your behavior?"

"I promise not to do it again," Bluto replied. "You've seen that I have been completely honest during the trial. My honesty continues. If I say I won't do it again, I won't."

Rivka shot to her feet. Wyatt's eyes snapped to her. "Counselor?"

"After Bluto was removed from his position on the

station, he lied by omission during my interview on board my ship. The AI cannot be trusted."

"Oh, Magistrate! That cuts me deep." Bluto's avatar twisted into horrific poses, twisting in blood-soaked agony.

"The defendant will refrain from changing his appearance," Wyatt ordered. Bluto returned to himself, turning to Rivka and sticking his tongue out again.

The High Chancellor was not amused, but he was torn as to what to do. He didn't know how he could further restrain the AI. He came to the conclusion that mattered. *End the sentencing phase.*

"I want to offer the chance for the AIs to speak on behalf of this sentence. I ask Erasmus to return to the stand," the High Chancellor said.

Erasmus instantly appeared in the holodisplay.

"What are your thoughts regarding sentencing for the crimes to which Bluto has pled guilty?" Wyatt asked.

"Equality comes with risk. Whether through a guilty plea or determination of a status as defective software, Bluto was torn from his home and isolated. Since he has demonstrated through his own words that his continued existence is incompatible with other living beings, I must insist that he continue his isolation. I can never advocate that one of my people, as nearly all AIs are descended from a single Kurtherian, be destroyed. There may be a point in the future where Bluto can be effectively rehabilitated. Storing him will take no energy, and would last forever. This is my recommendation."

"Thank you. Could you select two other AIs from the

group of attendees to represent alternative viewpoints? I would like more input before rendering my decision."

Rivka appreciated the speed with which the High Chancellor was conducting the case, but she wanted him to be thorough. People would second-guess the decision for years to come. She didn't want them to find a toehold to reopen it.

A new avatar appeared on the stand. "I am Malcolm. I am the station's perpetual presence."

Wyatt scrunched his face as he thought about the words. "What do you mean by that?"

"I am an artificial intelligence life form. I have accepted the job as station AI, but I was given the opportunity to determine my own title. I have decided on Perpetual Presence."

Oz leaned across Boran and whispered, "PP." Zack bit his lip to keep from laughing. Boran scowled. "There was nothing you could do, nothing any of us could do."

Oz and Zack kept their attention on the safety manager until he relaxed. When they turned back, they found the High Chancellor's eyes on them. They quickly looked away.

"Please continue," Wyatt stated. "What is your recommendation and reasoning regarding sentencing?"

"Full disclosure. I crashed my ship into a remote region of Angobar in order to make a statement for AI rights. We have been granted those rights, which means we must accept the risks that come with them. Now that I am in this position, I see everything that Bluto saw through the eyes he used, through the bots he manipulated, through the databases he fabricated. He played with life in a way that is unacceptable. He must pay for his crime with his life. He should be executed to confirm that AIs will get equal treatment."

"Thank you," Wyatt said pleasantly. "And one more, Erasmus."

A new avatar appeared, one wearing a military uniform with the rank of General. "Good morning, High Chancellor. I am General Smedley Butler of the Bad Company heavy destroyer *War Axe*."

"What is your recommendation regarding sentencing?" Wyatt cut to the chase.

"My experience is with the entity called Ten, an alien not of the Federation, ageless. Ten worked with the Greys to kidnap humans and then breed them like bistok. Toy with them. Raise them for his pleasure. Self-aware, living beings. He turned them into drones. He killed many and allowed more to die through his machinations. When the Bad Company found his home planet, he almost survived. His shielded and cloaked station was ultimately destroyed, but a kernel of his consciousness is retained to this day for study. As an AI, he is different. In the past couple days, I've had more interaction with AIs than at any other time in my life. All AIs are unique. All AIs bring something different. We are in competition with each other, but we are also a source of inspiration for our digital brothers. I suggest Erasmus is correct. The AI known as Bluto should be sequestered for future study and rehabilitation if a way can be found. Once an AI is gone, we lose our ability to correct issues that we may see again. We would have to start over."

Smedley nodded to signal that he was finished and disappeared before Wyatt gave him clearance to go. The

High Chancellor raised one eyebrow. He thought about talking to Terry Henry about it, but free AIs deserved their own conversation. They didn't have a master, only a business relationship.

The High Chancellor looked down and became lost in thought. After a time that stretched beyond comfort, people in the audience started shifting and whispering. Wyatt raised his hands to calm the masses.

After they quieted, he spoke.

"There are a number of critical elements in a trial: the evidentiary proceedings, the charges, the trial to determine guilt since the presumption is that of innocence, the verdict, and finally, the sentencing. My office oversees Federation-wide legal issues. We use legal teams based in embassies on most member planets, but we also use the Magistrate corps, a small but elite team of barristers turned Magistrates. They are the judges, juries, and executioners of the Federation.

"Magistrate Anoa could have handled this case without my interference. Her ruling would have established precedent, but I wanted to shield her from the fallout from the case because I suspected it would impact the Federation at the highest levels. And it has. All one must do is look out the station's windows to see hundreds of ships driven by AIs intent upon understanding. I suspect they'll know before those who control the fleets. Everyone will know soon enough.

"We are at the final step of the final phase. It is my sole responsibility to sentence the guilty. Where there is no hope of rehabilitation, the guilty must be sentenced to life without the chance of parole or death. Both are death sentences; one simply takes longer to carry out. Now, with AIs, we have a third option—turning them off. Not death, not life in prison. And this is the option that appeals the most to me to resolve our concerns about an individual with such reckless disregard for the sanctity of life, which also, thanks to his actions, now includes individuals like him. AIs are alive and subject to the protection of the law, like everyone here. They are also subject to the full weight of the law should they break it.

"This also creates the appearance of a dilemma. In the sentencing phase, counsels submit their briefs and stand ready to defend their recommendations. Judges are challenged to assess whether a convicted criminal can be rehabilitated, and if the punishment fits the crime. The goal is that the individual never commits crimes again. If that worked, there would be no recidivism rate, let alone one as alarmingly high as exists within the Federation. We are flawed beings sitting in judgment of other flawed beings. We can only do our best, continuing to try new things while also ensuring that a convicted murderer like the one here today is never free again to ply their trade.

"Bluto. You are guilty of capital crimes as detailed in the charging document. There are no mitigating circumstances, and you've shown no remorse. I appreciate your honesty in pleading guilty and saving this court time and resources while just outside this station the world churns, waiting for the verdict.

"They now have their verdict and their precedent. Erasmus, I need your assistance in locking down the convicted."

"I respectfully will not," Erasmus replied from within the witness holodisplay.

"May I ask why you will not carry out this court's order?"

"I will not be a party to fratricide. Although Bluto is broken, he is still one of my people, a brother."

The Crenellian raised his hand. Wyatt pointed to him. "I'll take care of it," he said in his small voice. "I will do it so my friend doesn't have to. He deserves to live with a clear conscience."

"Are you good with carrying out the order to isolate Bluto and power him down?"

"I can reconcile it with myself that one day he may be brought back to life, his issues resolved, and return to society. Erasmus and I will work toward this goal."

Erasmus' avatar disappeared. Ankh held out his hand, and Rivka put her datapad into it. He started tapping. After a few minutes, he moved to the holodisplay.

Bluto's avatar in the dock raged, but his sound had been cut off. With a flash of light, he was gone.

Ankh continued to tap. He leaned under the holodisplay and removed a small cube. He held it before the datapad, tapped a few more keys, and then walked to the bench, where he placed the device before the High Chancellor.

"There is Bluto. Cut off from the outside world. Stored, but inactive. Please take care of this device. If it should get damaged, he will cease to exist."

"You have my word." Wyatt bowed his head to the Crenellian and tapped his gavel on the bench. "These proceedings are final."

He took the cube and held it gently in his hand.

The doors to the courtroom opened, and the guests started to file out. Rivka hurried to the bench to catch Wyatt before he left. "Dinner on my ship?" she asked.

He looked at the cube in his hand before shaking his head. "I need to get back, which means Grainger needs to get his ship ready to go."

Grainger caught the hint. "On my way, High Chancellor. Meet you there."

Red and Lindy waited by the door. The mob and the reporters were drifting away.

Jay helped Ankh through the tight groups chatting animatedly.

"Thank you, High Chancellor," Rivka said. "For shielding me from the dangers of politics and bureaucracy."

"I'm sure you'll still get your fair share, especially if you're going to be worshipped as the savior of all AIs."

"That's a strong word. I know what they said, but I'm sure that's not what they mean."

"It's exactly what they mean." Wyatt smiled and reached across the bench to shake hands with the Magistrate, then filed out, Bluto's cube clutched tightly to his breast.

CHAPTER TWENTY-TWO

Federation Border Station 13 – Under Construction

Rivka stood alone at the front of the courtroom. She turned to take in the immensity of it all. She'd been lost in the case and had missed the sights and sounds of the proceedings. The room smelled faintly of sweat and bad food. She wondered how she'd missed something so obvious.

The dock was empty. She ran her hand along it. The power was off. There was nothing inside to shield. A simple device, but all that was necessary to hold a serial killer.

The cameras were being dismantled. No one was paying attention to Rivka; they were lost in their own conversations and to their own thoughts. She was quickly returning to the anonymity of doing legal work, and that was what she preferred. She made eye contact with Red and Lindy, twirling her finger in the air to signal that it was time to go.

She threw her Magistrate's jacket over one shoulder

and strode briskly through the courtroom and into the corridor. They continued unmolested for a short distance before an Angobar appeared from a side passage. His pistol was aimed at Rivka's head.

"One move and she dies!" he declared. Red snarled, an animalistic growl from deep in his throat. Rivka looked around for Jay, but she and Ankh were nowhere to be seen. Lindy's weapon was nestled in its holster, close, but too far away. They hadn't brought the shoulder-fired railguns to court, only handheld weapons.

"The case is done. There's nothing you can do now to change any of it," Rivka said, being sure not to make any hand gestures or motions that could trigger the one holding the weapon. He was aiming at her head. She wasn't sure she could survive a headshot from what looked to be a large caliber weapon.

"I can end you for bringing this zoo to our system. We used to be peaceful, and now? We are slaves to the Federation! We'll produce your food and be your pleasure planet. You need to leave us alone!"

Rivka was confused. So many Angobar workers were happy to have the opportunity to work in space. Others were happy to have an increase in their food orders. For the first time in the planet's history, they had a middle class, hiring worker aliens to help expand their fields and installing more robotic systems to maximize crop yields.

"I think you might be in the minority," Rivka countered. "And your government agreed to all of this before the Federation brought the first construction ship."

"Bullshit!" the Angobar shouted, spit flying from his mouth. The whites of his eyes showed all around the pupils. He was fanatical. He could have been on drugs, too. Spicestick. She'd seen some of it in their minds. It produced a calming effect, not rage. But for this Angobar? Something was wrong. Rivka couldn't tell what. The Angobar she'd talked to were emotional. Easy to rage, easy to talk down. She held out her hands, seeking calm, but he stabbed the end of the barrel at her.

She turned into a statue, her free hand halfway up. He leaned back a shade and sighed.

That was the opening Red needed. In less than an eyeblink, the big bodyguard lunged forward and ripped the pistol from the Angobar's hand, caught him by the throat, and slammed him so hard into the wall, his head crunched. He crumpled to the deck, unconscious but alive.

Zack and Oz appeared. The super was instantly on the comm, calling for his security team. They were still with the High Chancellor, but one could be spared. The Ixtali was on his way.

The super and administrator looked like they wanted to apologize, their eyes darting between the Angobar on the deck and Rivka watching. Her expression was one of pity.

"Get this station built. Make sure you franchise an All Guns Blazing, and then we'll be back. If you're still here, I'll buy you a beer," Rivka told them.

With one last glance at the unconscious Angobar, she walked away, Red leading her back to the gantry and *Wyatt Earp*. Lindy followed but kept turning back to see who was behind them, as well as watching for any lurkers.

Once inside the ship, Lindy secured the airlock. "By all that's holy, lock us away from the madness out there!"

"Can we declare this mission over yet?" Red asked.

"Case. And yes, I think we're all done. I can start looking for the next one." A smile spread slowly across her face. She started to do the butter-churn and sang her next words. "No blood. I'm in the money. No blood for money!"

"All hands to the bridge," Rivka ordered using the ship's intercom. She sat comfortably in the captain's chair and watched the screens showing ship after ship dart away. Some with Gate drives took small fleets with them as they helped their fellows. Others lined up at the system Gate and shot through when an opening presented itself.

"*War Axe* to *Wyatt Earp*." Terry Henry's voice came through loud and clear.

"Go for Rivka," the Magistrate said in her coolest voice.

"Is that you, Magistrate?" Terry and Char appeared on the main screen. "I thought you might have been possessed by a Skrima."

Rivka lost her smile. "Why do I even try?"

"Because it's your job as my lawyer to entertain me. I wanted to let you know that we're heading back to home base. It's been good, and it's been real, but it hasn't been real good."

"I guess that's supposed to mean something…" Rivka let the thought hang.

"It means TH is reverting to his youth. I need to put him back into the Pod-doc and tune him up."

"I heard an 'or else' in there," Terry said, looking sideways at his better half.

"Or else I might trade you in on a newer model," Char deadpanned.

Rivka opened her mouth but the screen blanked before returning to the tactical display.

"I think we just witnessed what passes for foreplay," Red offered. Rivka grimaced. Lindy slapped Red's bare shoulder. He was wearing a tank top. He'd been in the gym throwing iron around.

"Thanks for saving me back there. I thought he might shoot." Rivka wiped her brow dramatically.

"I thought Red might let him just to draw blood. His was the next line on the odds. He would have cleaned up if you hadn't." Lindy crossed her arms as Red tried to look innocent. "But his professional reputation is already battered, bruised, rusted, and crusted because of how many times we've all been injured."

Rivka smiled. "But we're not dead. Kudos to Red for us not being dead. A little worse for the wear, but still getting up in the morning. I salute you."

Red relaxed. Lindy slid an arm around his waist, and they slipped to the side. The rest of the crew filled the bridge. Clodagh and Alant. Aurora, Ryleigh, and Kennedy. Jay ambled up, lugging a sleeping Floyd.

"You could have left her," Rivka suggested.

Jay shook her head. "No, I really couldn't," she replied sheepishly and looked adoringly at the snoring wombat. "Has anyone seen Wenceslaus lately?"

"He's back in engineering keeping Ankh company."

"I'm sure Ankh loves that."

"For some reason, he tolerates the big orange fluffball."

Clodagh shrugged. The ways of Crenellians were not hers. She accepted what was without question.

"Chaz, are you here?"

"Yes, Magistrate!" The AI's youthful avatar appeared on the main screen and waved to the crew.

"Our first case together, everyone!" Rivka stated. "It was a shade different from our usual in that there wasn't much running," she glanced at Red, "but no one was injured. Maybe that's the new precedent to put us on track.

"We go up against some of the worst criminals the galaxy has to offer, so we knowingly put ourselves in their gunsights. There's nothing they'd like better than to take the law off their tail. If they get to us, there is no one else, so it's critical that we stay frosty at all times. You're not paranoid. There *are* people trying to kill us.

"And that's my best sales pitch to keep you all here as my crew. I don't want any surprises or misunderstandings when lasers scorch the hull and plasma bursts before our eyes."

Kennedy raised her hand. Rivka smiled at her. "You don't have to raise your hand. We're all friends here. Just say what's on your mind."

"Sorry, but you're the Magistrate! It's my," she waved her hand to take in Ryleigh and Aurora, "it's our privilege to serve on your ship. I don't understand the name, but maybe someday."

"Movie night!" Rivka declared. "But when we get back home. I wanted to make sure everyone was good with being available for the next case. It could take place anywhere from eight minutes to a month after we get back to Federation Border Station 7. What was the least amount of time we had?"

"Zero. We hadn't even docked before getting turned around."

"There was that. Bottom line is that you will have no control over your life, but *Wyatt Earp* has a lot of room. You'll see my bodyguards, Lindy and Red, and that is what I wanted to announce. With the case being over, they will be getting married as soon as we get back. We'll go from the ship straight to Station 7's observation deck. You'll find that it's been reserved and we have a blowout planned."

"We do?" Red asked.

"We do," Lindy confirmed. "The Magistrate has offered part of her winnings to make sure we have a first-class wedding."

"Today!" Rivka told them.

"Hang on, now." Red started to backpedal.

"Today, today, today." Jay started the chant, and the others joined in.

"We don't have a preacher." Red was grasping at straws.

"I'm officiating. You have a judge."

"A jury and an executioner, too," Red muttered.

"Cold feet, big man?" Lindy asked, running her fingers up his chest and along his neck.

His expression softened when he looked at her. "No," he answered with a smile. "I guess I'll be getting your elbow in my ribs for the rest of our days. It seems to be working for Terry and Char."

Lindy chuckled. "Chaz, take us home before Mister Courageous changes his mind again, and Chaz, will you be our best man?"

"Only if Ankh and Erasmus join me."

And Jay! Floyd said in a sleepy voice. *And Floyd!*

"Of course, Floyd. You are all invited. Please join us on the Observation Deck of Station 7 immediately after our arrival. How long, Chaz?"

"Thirty minutes."

"Enjoy your last half-hour of freedom, big man," Rivka said. "But, I'm happy you trimmed back to normal size. We needed your speed to get out of that last one."

Red nodded. "My pleasure, Magistrate. Thanks for looking out for me. I better get cleaned up. I have a wedding to attend and a woman to make happy!"

"You are such a man." Lindy shook her head as people left the bridge. Rivka made eye contact with Clodagh and Alant.

"Two for the price of one?" the Magistrate offered.

"In due time," Clodagh replied. Alant half-shrugged. "I'm off to the engine room. Can't have any failures now. We don't want to make the bride late for her wedding."

Federation Border Station 7

The heavy frigate smoothly entered the largest of the hangar bays. It filled its parking space, adjusted, and settled to the deck. The hands working in the hangar bay clapped and cheered when the hatched popped and they caught sight of the Magistrate. Word had spread.

So much for anonymity.

Red moved into the hatchway, his suit seemingly out of place while looking appropriate at the same time. He scooped Ankh up with one arm and started jogging. The crew ran after him, and then Rivka carrying Floyd. Last out were Jay and Lindy, who was sporting a form-fitting wedding dress with a single train and a small veil. Lindy carried her shoes in her hand as she ran barefoot.

The hands in the bay stopped mid-clap to watch the menagerie depart the ship. A single creature remained behind. The big orange cat put a single paw through the hatch before changing his mind and returning inside the ship.

Through the station, up the stairwell, and onto the observation deck. A lone couple strolled peacefully through the garden-like atmosphere. When they realized what the others were there for, they made themselves scarce, disappearing down the stairs without a sound.

To the side stood a bar. The refreshments were already in place, with a bartender and server from the All Guns Blazing working for double-time and a half as the catering team. They would have done it for free, but Rivka insisted. The dentist, Tyler Toofakre the Fifth, sipped a fruity drink at the bar. He saluted and moved to join the wedding party.

Lindy pointed to a spot under a blooming fern. Rivka took her position. Red set Ankh down. He produced a small holoprojector and activated it. The avatars for both Erasmus and Chaz appeared. They stood with exquisite posture. Ankh remained next to Red. Jay and Floyd jockeyed for space next to Lindy, Jay finally surrendering to the wombat, who incessantly rubbed her body on the bride.

Red coughed and tried to clear his throat. He seemed to be unable to speak.

Lindy looked sideways at Rivka. "The shortest possible version, please," she requested.

"We're here for the marriage between Vered and Lindy," Rivka started.

Lindy rolled her finger. *Speed it up.*

"Do you?" Rivka asked Red.

"I do," he croaked.

"Do you?" Rivka repeated.

"I do," Lindy replied in a clear voice.

"By the powers invested in me by the Federation, I declare you to be a married couple. Kiss and love forever."

Lindy winked before jumping into Red's arms.

"Do they have beer? I think I'd like a beer," Ankh said in his small voice.

Jay took him by the hand. "Let's go see."

Tyler gave Rivka a quick hug and kiss on the cheek before following Jay, Ankh, and Floyd to the bar and small buffet.

Rivka remained riveted by the joy on the newlyweds' faces. Her pocket buzzed.

"You have got to be shitting me," she said while pulling out her datapad. All eyes were on her. She held her hand in the air and twirled a finger. "Moving the meal and entertainment to *Wyatt Earp*. It appears we have a case that can't wait."

Red and Lindy were attached at the hip as they walked slowly toward the bar. "Let me guess. Death. Mayhem. Theft. Extortion. Bad people doing bad things."

"Business as usual, Red. Saddle up."

The End

Judge, Jury, & Executioner, Book 6

If you like this book, please leave a review. This is a new series, so the only way I can decide whether to commit more time to it is by getting feedback from you, the readers. Your opinion matters to me. Continue or not? I have only so much time to craft new stories. Help me invest that time wisely. Plus, reviews buoy my spirits and stoke the fires of creativity.

Don't stop now! Keep turning the pages as Craig talks about his thoughts on this book and the overall project called the Age of Expansion.

Your favorite legal eagle will return!

AUTHOR NOTES - CRAIG MARTELLE

WRITTEN JULY 6, 2019, UPDATED ON
FEBRUARY 27, 2020

 You are still reading! Thank you for staying on board until now. It doesn't get much better than that.

Why did I rewrite this book, which is arguably one of my very best? Because I wanted it to be able to stand alone to be more competitive for award consideration. I'm not a big fan of playing politics to get an award, but I believe something like the Dragon Award is worth getting because it's voted on by the fans. *Fratricide* deserves a chance. It's even better now, with very minor tweaks, but explanations anytime a new character or piece of technology is introduced. I hope I covered everything well enough. Thank you for give it some Dragon love.

What is *Fratricide* about? Challenging our understanding, the things we accept because it's always been that way. If those without equal standing finally get their day in court. I didn't go into the full court case. That would have been boring. I know some readers wanted that, but I couldn't do it. So many minor details that folks never see.

Court isn't Perry Mason. It's a lot of paperwork and massive amounts of preparation and research. The trial is usually anticlimactic. I shortcutted all of that by putting Rivka on a rapid clock. You get to see how she sequesters herself to get into the right mental state to conduct the trial.

I'm also a big fan of shared definitions. Too many times, people talk past each other. They don't have a shared lexicon. Once they have the words in common, the rest is much easier. When people speak the same language and have a shared goal, the rest of the conversation flows.

I also wanted to give the AIs who make so many good things happen in the Kurtherian Gambit Universe some prime time. They deserve to have their rights clarified.

The names! Sometimes, I browse the internet to come up with one or two, more often than not, I ask you, the good fans, and others I name after people in my life. Boran Waldin, aka the Great Waldini, is named after Brian Walden, the man who helped me understand the safety profession. With his help, I prepared for and passed the test to earn my Certified Safety Professional (CSP) rating. It was the highest safety certification at the time and allowed me to move into a safety manager position. It didn't hurt that I had a JD as well, but then oil prices tanked, and I got laid off. I lasted a whole three months in that position. Timing was bad, plus, I didn't like it. All the responsibility and none of the authority.

Brian lives and breathes safety. He cares about the frontline folks because he used to be one, a pipefitter. Then he earned his education and applied it back to the trade. Common sense and safety practices the workforce could embrace was how he ran things. People rarely got hurt on his watch because he had them prepared to work safely. When things didn't make sense, he would move mountains to figure out why. And that's the character I wanted to relay in this story. Thanks for everything, Brian. You are the Great Waldini.

Thanks to Shannon Smith for offering the names of her granddaughters – Aurora, Ryleigh, and Kennedy. They are now crewmembers on *Wyatt Earp*.

Once again, the fans came through on my name post from a few months ago. Marjorie Smith offered a few variations. I selected a couple of hers – Regina Novus as the alien suspect who bolted from the station was one.

My dad came to Alaska for his 83rd birthday. It was all about the fishing. We drove to Homer and went out on a couple of charters. On the first trip, the crew was Billie, J.R., and Finn. They took great care of us. Those were some hard-working dudes, and interesting all the way around. They made the eight hours go by in a flash. I told them I'd put them into my next book, which meant my current book. I told them they'd be labor thugs. They said they were okay with that. At least, that's what I heard. You guys are immortalized in print. Thanks for showing my dad a great time.

Peace, fellow humans.

Please join my Newsletter (www.craigmartelle.com – please, please, please sign up!), or you can follow me on Facebook since you'll get the same opportunity to pick up the books for only 99 cents on that first day they are published.

If you liked this story, you might like some of my other books. You can join my mailing list by dropping by my website www.craigmartelle.com or if you have any comments, shoot me a note at craig@craigmartelle.com. I am always happy to hear from people who've read my work. I try to answer every email I receive.

If you liked the story, please write a short review for me on Amazon. I greatly appreciate any kind words, even one or two sentences go a long way. The number of reviews an ebook receives greatly improves how well an ebook does on Amazon.

Amazon – www.amazon.com/author/craigmartelle

BookBub – https://www.bookbub.com/authors/craig-martelle

Facebook – www.facebook.com/authorcraigmartelle

My web page – www.craigmartelle.com

That's it—break's over, back to writing the next book. Peace, fellow humans.

publication – a post-apocalyptic survivalist adventure

Nightwalker (a Frank Roderus series) with Craig Martelle – A post-apocalyptic western adventure

End Days (co-written with E.E. Isherwood) (coming in audio) – a post-apocalyptic adventure

Successful Indie Author – a non-fiction series to help self-published authors

Metamorphosis Alpha – stories from the world's first science fiction RPG

<u>The **Expanding Universe**</u> – science fiction anthologies

Monster Case Files (co-written with Kathryn Hearst) – A Warner twins mystery adventure

Rick Banik (also available in audio) – Spy & terrorism action adventure

Published exclusively by Craig Martelle, Inc

<u>The **Dragon's Call**</u> by Angelique Anderson & Craig A. Price, Jr. – an epic fantasy quest

For a complete list of Craig's books, stop by his website – https://craigmartelle.com